The Treasure of Dubarry Castle

Lindsay Brown was only ten years old when she began to write this story and only twelve when it was published. The illustrator, Val Biro, has called it 'a remarkable achievement – it would do credit to an author of any age'.

Lindsay was born in Glasgow where she still lives, attending the Cleveden Secondary School and writing in her spare time.

Lindsay Brown

The Treasure
of Dubarry Castle

illustrated by Val Biro

Piccolo Books

for my dear brother, Rupert

First published 1978 by Robert Hale Ltd
This Piccolo edition published 1980 by Pan Books Ltd,
Cavaye Place, London SW10 9PG
2nd Printing 1981
© Lindsay Brown 1978
illustrations © Val Biro 1978
ISBN 0 330 26210 6
Printed and bound in Great Britain by
Richard Clay (The Chaucer Press) Ltd, Bungay, Suffolk

Contents

Author's note

I would like to express my gratitude to everyone who has given me help and encouragement in writing stories and in producing this book.

My thanks are due to all the teachers who have aided me in writing at Oakfield Nursery School, Kelvindale Primary School and Cleveden Secondary School. I am very grateful to Mr and Mrs Maurice Lindsay who read the book and arranged for it to be sent to Robert Hale Ltd, and to Gail Donaldson and Moira Luke who saw the story and mentioned it to Mrs Lindsay.

Mr John Hale has given me most helpful advice and encouragement at all times. I am also indebted to Mr Val Biro for producing the delightful illustrations and the jacket design, all of which show the characters just as I had imagined them.

Many of my relations have helped in various ways, especially my parents, and Mrs Susan White kindly typed out the story for me.

To all those who have been mentioned and who have assisted or encouraged me, I am extremely grateful.

chapter one

Sarah and the Thomas family

'Sarah!' Mrs Parkinson called her daughter as she
sat in the kitchen with an opened air mail envelope
and a letter on the table beside her. Sarah, a fair-
haired girl with blue eyes, aged eleven, came downstairs to see what her mother wanted. Mrs Parkinson
looked pale and spoke in an anxious voice. 'Sarah,
dear! I have just received a letter from Canada
where my sister, Harriet, lives. She is very ill and I
must go to her as soon as possible. I'm afraid, dear,
you will have to stay at home as it would mean
missing school if you came with me. Would you like
to stay with the Thomas family if I could arrange
it? They moved in a few months ago. I have made
friends with Mrs Thomas and she seems an extremely nice woman. The Thomases, you see, are
the only people in the village with children although I don't know what they are like; but if the
rest of the family are as kind as Mrs Thomas, you
should have quite a good time. And you see,' –
in a miserable, worried voice – 'I – I don't know
of anyone else to ask. Sarah, I know it's all very
sudden and that you haven't much choice but – but,
well I – er—'

'Don't worry. I shan't mind so long as Aunt

Harriet recovers soon,' said Sarah coming to the rescue.

Her mother smiled weakly. 'Good girl! But you do understand, don't you? It wouldn't be much fun for you with Aunt Harriet so poorly. It will all be very expensive, but I shall have to manage.'

Sarah's father had died four months before she was born and since then money had been scarce for Mrs Parkinson and her only child. But the hard-working woman earned enough money to provide sufficient food and clothes for Sarah and herself.

'How long will you be away?' asked Sarah, a little downcast at losing her beloved mother.

'Oh! I couldn't tell you,' replied Mrs Parkinson. 'Maybe as long as three weeks, but, of course, I shall write to let you know when I get there. I shall be staying in your Aunt's flat.'

'Poor Aunt Harriet!' moaned Sarah. 'Send her my love.'

When Sarah came home from school the next day her mother said that she had spoken to Mrs Thomas and it was all arranged. Mrs Thomas was pleased to have Sarah, and there was now only one day until Mrs Parkinson left.

On Friday evening Sarah and her mother packed their things, trying to cram as much as possible into the only two suitcases they had.

Saturday morning came and the plane for Canada was due off at eleven o'clock. After a hasty breakfast, Sarah's mother phoned for a taxi. Then she walked with her daughter up the road to the Thomases' house.

Mrs Parkinson's small figure slowly disappeared down the road

Mrs Thomas greeted them at the door. Sarah liked the look of the kindly face surrounded by short, fluffy, yellow hair and with small bright eyes and a welcoming smile.

'So you're Sarah?' she said, patting the girl's shoulder. 'Come on in, dear. Let me take your case.'

'I'm afraid I must go quickly and meet my taxi,' announced Mrs Parkinson. 'And let me say once more how grateful I am to you for having Sarah.' Then came the 'goodbyes', and Sarah couldn't stop tears from gushing out as she flung her arms round her mother. Mrs Thomas was very comforting when Mrs Parkinson's small figure slowly disappeared down the road.

Sarah was ushered into the house, and while she was hanging up her coat an untidy girl came thundering down the stairs with her brown hair streaming behind her. She stopped in the hall and stood staring at Sarah.

'This is Molly,' said Mrs Thomas. 'Say "hello", Molly!'

'Hello,' smiled Sarah. The same words squeezed out unwillingly from between Molly's thick pursed lips.

'Molly, take Sarah to her room,' said Mrs Thomas. Molly frowned so that her freckled nose was screwed up. She did not seem to like her visitor. Molly eventually turned and bounded up the stairs. She was a plump girl squeezed into a green, checked dress with a dirty pink cardigan slipped over it. Molly's fat face looked down at Sarah over her shoulder.

'Well, c'me on then,' she ordered in a loud, husky voice. Sarah lifted her suitcase and followed. Her room was pretty with a small bed fitted into one corner, one large window and a low roof. Two grubby boys aged about six and eight were standing by the wardrobe, quarrelling.

'Mum said you were to get out a towel for the girl that's coming,' the older one was saying.

'No, she said *you* had to,' squealed the younger.

'Little liar!' screeched the big boy. 'You're a lazybones, Mark!'

'Am not, Billy! You've to get a towel,' argued Mark.

'Shove off, you two!' interrupted Molly as she strode in, leaving Sarah standing nervously at the door.

'Nay,' retorted Billy, and ducked as Molly tried to cuff his ear. The two boys sauntered out. Billy stuck a fat pink tongue out at his sister as he left the room, and Mark laughed loudly.

'Well, this is your room,' said Molly. 'Wait till I get that little devil, Billy!' With that she rushed wildly from the room, slamming the door behind her.

Sarah opened the wardrobe door to hang up her clothes but she found that someone else's coat and shoes were inside. Just then Mrs Thomas poked her head through the door, smiling.

'Getting on all right?' she asked.

'Er – where should I put my things?' queried Sarah.

'Why, in the wardrobe of course.'

'But someone else is using it.'

Mrs Thomas sighed wearily after looking in the wardrobe. 'These are Billy's things. He usually uses this wardrobe and I told him to take his things out. He is a very disobedient boy. *Billy,* come here!' There was no answer. 'BILLY!' yelled Mrs Thomas. There was the noise of running feet up the stairs and Billy came into the room. Mrs Thomas looked at her disgraceful son in horror. His dark hair was tangled up with some sort of sticky stuff and hung loosely touching his shirt collar. His grey tie was crooked and dangled next to a row of shirt buttons which were all undone. His yellow pullover was smudged with jam stains, not to mention a dirty mark where he had dropped a liquorice sweet, and a hole in the elbow of his sleeve. His face was filthy, with dirty streaks across his forehead, a running nose, and a mouth which was surrounded by a circle of sticky jam. His beady eyes stared at a dirty hand clutching half a candy stick. His pair of torn grey shorts had loose white threads hanging down. His knees were almost black with dirt and one of his socks, which was smeared with grease, had fallen down, touching a black shoe which was muddy and had the laces undone.

'Billy! You've been eating jam!' scolded Mrs Thomas.

'Why not? There were two pots in the larder and you only need one so I ate the other.'

'You bad boy! And what did I tell you to do with these shoes and your coat?'

Billy shrugged. 'Don't know! Wasn't listenin'.'

'Well, I told you to put your shoes under your bed and—'

'There isn't room! All my toys and games are there.'

'There is plenty of room and you know it.' Billy scowled but Mrs Thomas ignored him and went on, 'And I told you to hang your coat in the hall. Really, Billy! It's too bad!'

'It's not! Anyway, I'm busy! I'm playing cars in the garden so why don't you do it for me?' He stalked out, sucking his candy, and galloped downstairs.

'Billy! You come right back here!' shouted Mrs Thomas, but her son took no notice. Sighing, the woman lifted Billy's things out of the wardrobe. 'I do apologize,' she said to the horrified Sarah. 'They always try to show off when we have visitors.' Sarah could not imagine where the Thomas children got their bad manners from. Mrs Thomas was so nice and kind!

The weary mother stopped at the door with the coat and shoes. 'When you've put your clothes away come down for a morning snack.'

The 'morning snack' consisted of cream buns and an appetizing selection of biscuits. All four children turned up for the food and the Thomas children ate like pigs. When they had satisfied their appetites, Molly, Billy and Mark went into the garden. It was midsummer and the June sun was very warm. Sarah felt lonely. She had hoped that the Thomas children would play with her. However, she went to her room and read a book with the shouts of Molly,

Billy and Mark from the garden ringing in her ears. At eleven o'clock she looked at her watch and thought of her mother just setting off on the plane to Canada.

Later on she heard a vehicle coming up the drive and shouts of glee from the children. Looking out of the window, she saw that it was an expensive-looking cream-coloured car. A man inside drove it into the garage and locked the door. The Thomas children ran to the tall man crying 'Daddy, Daddy!' That made Sarah sigh, wishing she had a father. Mr Thomas carried Mark into the house on his shoulders.

'I'm getting a piggy-back!' chanted Mark, boasting to his big brother. Mr Thomas chatted to his children who evidently preferred him to their mother.

'Hello, Alfred dear,' Sarah heard Mrs Thomas say to her husband, taking his briefcase and placing it in a corner of the hall from where their voices drifted upstairs.

'Oh, hullo,' grunted Mr Thomas not seeming too pleased at meeting his wife. 'Where's my lunch?'

'It's ready and waiting. *Children!* LUNCH!'

Sarah descended to the dining-room. She felt shy as she entered and met Mr Thomas for the first time at close quarters. He was a tall, broad man with hefty shoulders and thin dark hair swept away from his forehead. There was a small, neat brown moustache above his thin curved lips and his nose was narrow. Two small eyes fitted under a pair of bristly eyebrows.

Mr Thomas looked her up and down

'Is this – what's-her-name – oh yes, Sarah?' he asked gruffly.

'Yes, dear – Sarah Parkinson,' replied his wife. Sarah smiled nervously and felt embarrassed as Mr Thomas looked her up and down without even saying 'How do you do?' Soon they were all sitting round the table enjoying a tasty meal of steak and kidney pie. In their father's presence the Thomas children 'showed off' tremendously. They gnawed their meat with their mouths open at the same time as giggling. Mr Thomas grinned to see them cramming food into their mouths. Billy and Mark were seeing who could make the most revolting noise with a glass of orangeade and a straw.

'Oh, really! Now stop that or—' began Mrs Thomas.

'Oh, leave 'em alone,' interrupted her husband.

'But they are disgusting,' moaned poor Mrs Thomas. 'Look how nicely Sarah eats.'

Her husband grunted and plunged his fork into a roast potato.

After lunch Sarah helped to wash the dishes. Mrs Thomas told Molly to play a game of 'Scrabble' with Sarah. The fat ten-year-old girl got out the playing board and bag of Scrabble letters. But Sarah could see that Molly kept cheating by peeping into the bag to pick out the letters she wanted; so it was not surprising that the unpleasant Thomas girl won. For the rest of the afternoon Sarah felt bored. Mr Thomas had his radio on as loud as it would go, to listen to the horse-racing results. The three children were in the garden and Mrs Thomas had gone to the shops, so Sarah was all alone again. Eventually she went upstairs and read her book all over again until supper time. She hopped into bed early because she had nothing else to do.

On Sunday morning the sun streamed through the bedroom window and her eyes flickered open. She went down for breakfast. Mr Thomas was opposite her at the table. His checked dressing-gown was tied at the waist by a cord and his feet were tucked into floppy red slippers. His face was buried in the morning newspaper and he sat there for so long, struggling over a difficult crossword, that his porridge went cold. Sarah was tired of having the paper right in front of her with some rubbish about valuable watches that had been stolen from a jeweller's shop written across the first page.

After breakfast Sarah told herself, 'It's no use just sitting around all day doing nothing. I shall have to make friends with those Thomas children. If I am nice to them they are bound to let me join in their games.' So she went out into the garden where Molly, Billy and Mark were playing with a ball.

'Hello!' she called striding over. To her surprise they stopped throwing the ball and scowled at her. 'What's wrong? I thought you might let me join in your game. Do you mind?'

'Don't want to play with *you*,' growled Molly. 'You're stuck-up. Bet you wouldn't climb over that wall and back again.'

'Of course I wouldn't! My clothes would get dirty

and torn on those prickly bushes. Besides, there's a big muddy patch there and I've got my best shoes on.'

'See! You're too posh and proud. Stuck-up! Go away 'cos we're not playing with you!'

Mark and Billy stuck their tongues out as Sarah trudged miserably back to the house. It was too bad! The girl was too shy to go back to argue. It wouldn't be any fun playing with them if they didn't want her anyway.

In the afternoon Molly, Billy and Mark watched a ghastly cartoon on television which was noisy and cruel with ridiculous characters. At teatime, Mr Thomas listened with glee to the tricks his children intended to play on their teachers at school the following week. Except at mealtimes, Mrs Thomas was Sarah's only companion throughout the day. The kind woman let Sarah help with the house-work and listen to some records.

When Sarah switched off her light at nine o'clock that evening, she lay in bed thinking about this family she had come to stay with. Mrs Thomas was kind and friendly but Mr Thomas encouraged his children in their rude and mischievous ways.

chapter two

A friend at last

Monday morning brought the start of a new school week. Sarah and the Thomas children attended Rockfield School, which stood in the neighbouring village where most of the pupils lived. Mrs Thomas came into Sarah's room at half past seven and drew back the curtains. Sarah blinked and sat up.

'Breakfast in fifteen minutes!' called Mrs Thomas as she went out. Sarah yawned and climbed out of bed.

As she went downstairs to breakfast, dressed in her grey school uniform, she heard Billy, Molly and Mark shouting and arguing while they got washed and dressed. Mr Thomas seemed to be in a bad mood that morning, so Sarah ate her porridge quietly and succeeded in avoiding him. He was smoking a filthy pipe, which filled the room with coils of smoke. When Mrs Thomas asked him to put it away, he only snapped at her and pored over the sports pages in his morning paper.

Sarah left for school at half past eight. Mrs Thomas had told her to hurry on ahead as Billy, Molly and Mark were very late finishing their breakfast. Halfway to school, she didn't realize that the Thomas children had caught up behind her until a menacing voice squawked, 'All alone, then? No friends? What a shame, eh!'

Sarah turned to see Billy staring at her mockingly. She walked on with her back to him, hot with anger, but too afraid to shout back. Another sarcastic voice, Molly's this time, cried, 'I suppose you're so high and mighty that no one's good enough to be your friend!'

A chorus of giggles was followed by whispering, and then Billy called, 'You're so posh that if you have a friend she must be perfect – someone who never does a thing wrong – full marks for all her tests – the pride of all the teachers! No one is good enough for you. Ha! Ha!'

Sarah blinked back the tears as her eyes brimmed. 'You must have a wonderful friend who is perfect. No one is fit for you. It must be a friend who ...'

Sarah didn't stop to hear any more. She rushed down the road, glad that those three pests weren't chasing her. She arrived breathless in the school playground, and rested against the wall with wet cheeks. She thought hard. It was true that she had no friends, but that wasn't because no one was good enough for her. Any friend would do, but she just couldn't seem to make one. This was surprising, because Sarah was a kind girl, with a quick brain. Everyone else seemed to have their own special friend. She had hoped to become friendly with the Thomas children, but she could see that there was no chance of this. Sarah could remember a friend she had had until the end of the previous year, called Susan Charles. She had been a merry, kind

Sarah didn't stop to hear any more

playmate. Sarah and Susan had gone everywhere and done almost everything together. But Susan had left Rockfield School to go and live in America. She had been such a good friend. How Sarah missed her! She had been ... The shrill ringing of the school bell interrupted Sarah's daydreams, and the children scurried into their school. Today, because her mother didn't want Mrs Thomas to go to too much trouble with meals, Sarah was having school lunches for the first time. She liked school, and enjoyed her morning lessons, but at the interval she stood by herself, lonely and rather sad. When Molly came by, with her friend Caroline, she taunted Sarah, who turned away angrily.

At lunch time, she entered the dinner hall, shy in front of all the children who were chatting away merrily. The woman in charge gave Sarah a seat opposite a dark-haired girl wearing glasses with thick lenses and announced, 'This is Deborah.'

Sarah thought gladly, 'Perhaps I can make friends with Deborah. She looks quite lonely.' Sarah spoke aloud and said with a beaming smile, 'Hello.'

But Deborah screwed up her freckled face angrily. She spoke coldly. 'What are you smiling at, you beast? Never seen anyone wearing glasses before?'

Looking very upset, Deborah saw the dinner lady signalling and went over to the food counter. Sarah followed, shy and disappointed. 'I wasn't laughing at Deborah's glasses. I was only trying to be pleasant,' she thought, biting her lip. 'Deborah's a horrid girl. Why won't anyone be my friend? It's too bad!'

She sniffed as she carried a plate of meat and mashed potatoes to her seat. She didn't find the school lunches as horrid as some of the children said they were, but preferred her mother's own meals at home.

During her afternoon classes, her mind wandered as she thought of her mother in Canada, and of Aunt Harriet, and wondered how they were getting on. After school, she wrote a long letter to her mother and went to post it that evening.

Next morning, at nine o'clock as usual, Sarah's form crowded into their classroom, waiting for their teacher, the tall, prim Miss Hunter, to arrive. It wasn't long before they realized that a newcomer was hovering about by the teacher's desk. He was handsome, with dark glossy hair, brown nervous eyes and a well-built, quite tall body. He was smart in his new grey blazer, and carried a shiny briefcase. A whole lot of curious glances were cast upon the strange boy, and he looked very uncomfortable. Suddenly Miss Hunter's footsteps were heard in the corridor, and all but the new boy scampered to their seats. Miss Hunter stalked in, said something quietly to the boy by her desk, and then announced to the class, 'This is Jack Wilton, a new member for this class. I hope you will all welcome him nicely.' Her eyes looked round for a responsible person. 'Sarah! You will take care of Jack on his first day. Show him where the cloakrooms, the gymnasium and so on are.'

Sarah's heart leapt. Was she to have a friend at last? Jack looked nice. Was he? Or was he like Mark and Billy? Would he just think she was a soppy girl? Masses of questions whirled through Sarah's mind as she led Jack to the cloakroom. She had never thought of having a boy as a friend, but ... it was merely the same as knowing a girl. Jack was nice to her and spoke cheerily. He liked Sarah because she was quiet and pretty.

At the interval, Jack wandered off on his own. Sarah watched alone from a distance. Then she began to wonder if Jack wanted her as a friend. After all, she *was* a girl, and she had only been showing him round the school. But Jack wandered over to her, as he was lonely. He smiled and said, 'Tell me more about your school.'

Sarah proceeded happily.

Jack proved a great success in his new class. He was top in the week's maths and English tests. In the gymnasium, he climbed ropes like a monkey, vaulted easily over bars and hurdles, and was excellent at netball. He played the piano very well, much to the delight of his music teacher. But the other boys were very jealous of him, especially the malicious Robert Simpson who had been top in all classes before Jack arrived; so Jack couldn't make friends with any of the male class members. That is why he stuck to the pretty, admiring Sarah. Because Jack had a girl as a friend, Robert was given a chance to tease his new rival. Robert and his playmates all plotted together to find ways of tormenting the new boy, whom they regarded as a 'conceited show-off'. They wouldn't let Jack join in when they played football; they only told him to 'Go away and

Robert laughed at him and called him a coward

get married to Sarah Parkinson'. Robert wrote on the back of Jack's English jotter 'Jack Wilton is a snob'. His friend Terry added in red ink 'Jack Wilton loves Sarah Parkinson'. If Robert met Jack alone in the corridor, he would kick him, but Jack would never kick back, even when Robert laughed at him and called him a coward. Jack knew that he wasn't afraid of Robert Simpson, but Jack wanted as little to do with Robert as possible.

But one afternoon Miss Hunter discovered, and recognized, the untidy handwriting on the back of Jack's English jotter. Later on that day, she happened to walk round a corner in the corridor and to catch Robert and his friends kicking Jack. Miss Hunter was very angry and gave each of the culprits one hundred lines, two hours' detention and a severe warning, which put an end to their spiteful pranks.

At the end of his first week at Rockfield School, Jack invited Sarah to his house for tea on Friday. Jack had just moved into the same village as Sarah, so it didn't take her long to get to his house from the Thomases'. Mrs Wilton was a dark-haired woman as cheerful as her son. She had laid the table with cakes, buns and biscuits. Yvonne, Jack's sister, who was a little younger than Sarah, joined them in the tasty meal. Sarah thought the Wiltons were extremely nice, polite, cheerful people, a big change from Mr Thomas and his quarrelsome, unfriendly children. As new wallpaper was being hung upstairs, the children had to play outside. Mrs Wilton suggested that they got out Jack's inflatable paddling pool, and Yvonne could lend Sarah her swimming costume. Sarah thought that was very decent of Yvonne, because Jack's sister had only one costume and so wasn't able to play in the pool herself. Yvonne sat and watched goodheartedly, laughing as Jack and Sarah kicked water over each other. A black cat was stretched out lazily on a nearby wall. She jumped up as she was sprinkled with water.

'Watch out! You've splashed the cat!' said Sarah.

'Oh, that's my pet, Samantha,' laughed Jack. 'She can't stand getting drenched, but doesn't mind being splashed. If the bath tap's dripping, she sits with her paw underneath, so that water drips on to it.'

Sarah laughed, and threw a bucketful of cold water over her friend.

'Ooh, you beast!' cried Jack, and he sprayed Sarah with the garden hose they had been playing with.

It was a very enjoyable afternoon, and Sarah was so glad that she had made a good friend at last.

chapter three

The circus

Saturday morning bloomed bright and fair. Sarah
awoke to hear shouting and jumbled voices coming
from outside. Her room looked out over a wide
stretch of empty fields which lay at the back of the
village houses and were hardly visited by anyone.
Sarah got up and peeped through the curtains,
blinking at first in the dazzling sunlight. In the
field behind the Thomases' house a mass òf people
and caravans had appeared overnight. At first Sarah
thought they were gypsies but then she saw these
words painted on one caravan in gay letters:
'MISTER MORGAN'S TRAVELLING CIRCUS'.
Sarah leapt for joy. She had never seen a circus
before. The circus folk were wearing their ordinary
clothes – ragged shirts and jeans. There was a delightful odour of sausages cooking as some of the
old women held pans over wood fires. Sarah stood
and stared. She could see circus children aimlessly
wandering around with chunks of bread and sausages. Some men were fascinating to watch as they
practised cartwheels, hand-stands and fancy somer-
saults. Most of the caravans were painted gaily and
a monkey was poised on top of one. To Sarah's

delight a little boy waved at her and she did the same. Just then Mrs Thomas came in.

'Good morning,' she said. 'Nice day, isn't it?'

'Yes,' agreed Sarah. 'Did you know there is a circus in the fields?'

'Yes,' replied Mrs Thomas. 'It's Mr Morgan's. I think they came to the village where we lived before we moved here.' She smiled. 'I know that you would like to gaze all day, but please come and have breakfast; then afterwards you can dress, go outside and watch the circus.'

'Right,' said Sarah.

Molly, Billy and Mark were still in the house having breakfast when Sarah skipped outside to watch the circus activities. There were several lorries with cages on the back. Some of these cages were covered up but a few were not and Sarah was able to look at the animals inside. Breakfast was over for the circus folk and a lot of strong men were hoisting up poles to put up a huge coloured tent or Big Top. Sarah stood for nearly twenty minutes watching the red and blue canvas tent being set up. Suddenly a dirty black and white dog with frizzled fur ran by yelping, and an equally grubby ginger-haired boy raced after it screeching, 'Rags, Rags, come here, boy! RAGS!' The dog didn't pay any attention. 'RAGS! RAGS!' yelled the boy.

Mr Thomas, still in his bedroom trying to sleep, could stand the noise no longer. He flung open the window, stuck out a ferocious face and cried, 'SHUT UP! Some people are trying to sleep!

Drat you! Noise! Noise! Noise! Shut up and let me sleep!'

A deathly hush had gradually fallen over the circus, but when Mr Thomas had shut the window and climbed back into bed the circus folk began to mutter in low voices about the rude man who had appeared in pyjamas and insulted their circus. A grubby, fierce-looking man threw a pebble at Mr Thomas' bedroom window and called, 'Just watch who you're talking to, you mean old pig!'

Mr Thomas rose from beneath the blankets, red with fury, and, flinging the window open with such force that it nearly flew off its hinges, screamed, 'How dare you? You hostile, ignorant, insolent ruffian! How dare you? Get out of my sight or I'll get the p'lice on to you!'

'Now look here—' began a man in smart clothes, who looked like a ringmaster, but Mr Thomas had slammed the window shut to hear the irritating voice of his wife calling, 'Alfred, aren't you ever coming down for breakfast?'

Meanwhile the circus folk had decided to move all their lorries and caravans a little way up the field. They didn't like camping right next to the unpleasant Mr Thomas. All the caravans were pulled by lorries and horses from the left side of the Big Top to the right, with a loud clanking of wooden wagon wheels. Just then Molly, Billy and Mark came running out to see the circus. They had dressed untidily in their hurry to get outside.

'Look! Oh look – a tent!' cried Billy.

'A monkey!' shouted Mark.

They wandered between the bright wagons

'There's an elephant in that cage!' exclaimed Molly.

The three children annoyed the circus folk by racing around and getting in everyone's way. They interfered with anything they could get their hands on, so it was not surprising that the angry people sent them away. Sarah, hovering shyly in the background, thought that she had better go too. When she got back into the house she was delighted to find that a letter had come for her from Canada. It was from her mother, of course, and told of her safe arrival. She said that she would be sending a longer letter later.

On Monday, after school, Sarah met Jack and they decided to have a look round the circus together. The sun beat down on them as they wandered between the bright wagons watching the circus folk prepare for their first show which was that day. They saw a procession of poodles being led towards the Big Top by a lady in a frilly skirt. Suddenly Jack said, 'My family are coming to tomorrow's performance here and my mother said she would like it if you could come too.'

'Oh, how lovely!' exclaimed Sarah. 'I do hope Mrs Thomas lets me.'

'So do I,' agreed Jack. 'Oh, look over there – two chimps!'

Jack was right. A handsome man was leading the chimpanzees out of a big caravan. One of the animals saw Jack and came lolloping over in his white T-shirt and blue shorts. He seemed to like Jack and the boy was delighted when two hairy black arms hugged him and the orange eyes in the sweet monkey face looked up at him. The chimpanzee's owner strode over, smiling. He produced a banana and threw it to the animal which was embracing Jack. Very soon the banana was peeled and demolished.

The chimpanzee owner was holding the paw of another ape who was wearing a blue skirt with her white T-shirt. This little creature whimpered and looked enquiringly at its master.

'All right, here's one for you too, you little rascal,' he said, tickling the ape's chin and putting a tasty banana into her greedy paw. The handsome man turned to Jack.

'Ha! Ha!' he laughed. 'My chimp, Gepetto, likes you, young lad. This one here' – pointing to the one in the skirt – 'is his sister Jessica.'

Jack smiled politely and kissed Gepetto's nose.

'Are you coming to the show today?' asked the chimpanzee owner.

'No, we're coming tomorrow,' answered Jack. 'This is Sarah, by the way. She is so quiet that you probably didn't notice her.'

Sarah smiled and the man laughed cheerfully. 'Well, I'm called Lianio,' he said. 'Come on, Gepetto, leave that poor boy alone.'

Gepetto and Jessica were led away reluctantly by Lianio who gave Sarah and Jack a friendly wink.

'Isn't Lianio a funny name?' said Sarah to Jack as they watched the man and his chimpanzees disappear into the tent.

'It's a circus name,' said Jack in reply. 'They

always have fancy names in circuses. It's probably not his real name. His real name would be a plain one like Bill Jones or Dick Smith, but it sounds rather boring if you say "And now here is Bill Jones with his chimpanzees" – it's much more exciting to say "Here is Lianio with his chimpanzees".'

Sarah admired her friend's knowledge. Her eyes wandered across the field and she saw a massive elephant being led out of a cage. Sarah followed Jack as he ran over. A strong man led the elephant and a pretty woman in a pink and silver costume walked beside it. Jack, with Sarah behind him, approached the woman calling cheerily, 'Hello there! Magnificent animal you've got!'

Jack's handsome face and merry voice made him a likeable boy and nearly everyone he met was friendly towards him. The woman smiled at Jack's remark.

'Yes, she is nice, isn't she? I ride her.'

'Smashing!' said Jack, who was by now skipping along beside the woman with the shy Sarah at his side. 'What's her name?'

'I call her Celia.' The woman patted Celia's side. 'Whoa there! Up-hoay! Good girl!'

The elephant's trunk had coiled round the pretty woman's waist and lifted her on to its broad back. The woman waved as she was carried towards the Big Top. Jack and Sarah stood and watched Celia as the big animal lumbered along with bells jingling round its legs and feathery plumes swishing between its ears. In less than an hour the show would begin and all the performers were busy preparing for it. Clowns painted on make-up, acrobats warmed up and slipped into their gay costumes, horses and ponies cantered around the field adorned with gay ribbons and bells. The band could be heard practising and the Ringmaster in a red tailcoat and a shiny top hat strode about. But the Ringmaster looked worried and agitated. So did quite a few other folk who hovered about nervously as if waiting for something.

'They're late, they're late!' muttered the Ringmaster anxiously, and some others added, 'Where are they? They should have arrived ages ago!'

Mobs of circus entertainers, acrobats, clowns in baggy trousers, trapeze artists and animals with their trainers trailed into the huge tent. A group of sealions, sleek and black, were led in by a woman carrying coloured balls for them to balance on their noses. But something was wrong! Someone was late!

A man passed Jack and Sarah, juggling dishes and balls as he went.

'By Jove – that's clever!' exclaimed Jack. The juggler heard and turned a grinning face on the boy. By doing this he dropped two balls and a dish. That made the two children and the juggler laugh.

'Ha! I'm not so clever after all!' smiled the man, picking up his equipment.

'Mountjoy – is that your name?' asked Jack, reading the gay letters across the front of the juggler's suit.

'That's right,' said Mountjoy in a friendly manner. 'I'm the son of Mr Morgan. My father owns this circus. He's very old and hardly ever leaves our caravan, so I have to do a lot of the arranging. They say that soon he won't wake up one morning, poor father – no wonder, though, he's ninety-two! Well, I must be getting along. Cheerio!' Mountjoy walked off, juggling as he did so.

'Nice chap!' said Jack to Sarah, and the couple strolled on. Suddenly a circus girl came running past, bumped into Sarah, and knocked her accidentally on to the ground where there was a muddy patch.

'You OK?' asked the circus girl, helping Sarah to her feet.

'I'm fine, but I'm dirty,' replied Sarah, examining the smears of mud streaking her best red skirt. Somehow they had got into a large crowd and Sarah had lost Jack.

'I'm sorry,' said the circus girl. 'Do you want my Ma to clean you up? She's awfully particular 'bout me running into folks.'

'It's all right – I must find my friend Jack,' replied Sarah.

'I'll help you,' said the girl, anxious to make amends after knocking down Sarah. They squeezed out of the crowd and soon enough Sarah spied Jack not far off.

'Hello!' he said. 'Who's your friend, Sarah?'

'I'm Anna,' announced the girl. 'Look what I've done to your chum's skirt!'

'I've told you – it doesn't matter!' laughed Sarah. She liked Anna with her sunburned, freckled, friendly face and almost black, rather straggly hair, which dangled down just touching her shoulders. Anna's black eyes gleamed as she said, 'Well, I must be off to groom Mr Jimminy's horse, Sasha. Want to come and watch?'

'Rather!'

'Yes, please!'

The horse was a beautiful glossy brown with a splendid saddle, a really charming, gentle creature, unlike its owner Mr Jimminy with his black hair, little moustache, pointed beard and malevolent dark eyes. He scolded and snapped at Anna as she decorated Sasha with bells and ribbons. Mr Jimminy wore a glittering costume, half blue and half yellow, and when his horse was ready he lifted a shiny whip, mounted, and galloped away.

'Crotchety old thing!' thought Sarah. 'He didn't even thank Anna.'

Their circus friend walked over grinning. 'Super horse!' she said.

'Yes, but not too nice an owner!' added Jack.

With only slightly more than forty minutes before the show, Anna had many last minute jobs to do. She helped the women to get into their tight costumes, fetched a clown some extra make-up, chased after a runaway poodle and took a costume, which had torn at the last minute, to her Ma's caravan. Jack and Sarah went with her, and Anna told them that her Ma was in charge of many costumes and made most of the outfits. Inside Anna's caravan piles of cotton reels, sequins, ribbons, lace, gold buttons and silver braid were strewn everywhere as Anna's Ma made last minute adjustments to things. Jack and Sarah stood outside while Anna entered the caravan. Ten minutes later she popped out wearing a gorgeous white frock adorned with yellow velvet ribbon. Her black hair had been brushed out so that it shone and her face was clean and pretty. She laughed at the astonished faces of Sarah and Jack.

'Are you performing?' asked Sarah.

'No, I'm just selling programmes. I can't do that all messy and in dirty clothes. I must go and collect my programmes now.'

'You look smashing!' said Jack, remembering his manners.

'Thanks!' grinned Anna. 'Hey! Coming to the show tonight? I could get you free tickets.'

Sarah's and Jack's hearts leapt, but Jack remembered and said, 'That's very kind, but my father has bought tickets for us all to come tomorrow.'

'Oh!' said Anna, and racked her brains for some other generous offer. 'Well, how about coming to my caravan for supper tomorrow after you have seen the show? My parents will both be out. They are going to dine with Mountjoy and Mr Morgan. It's a great honour for them.'

'Ooh, we'd love to come!' said Sarah. 'We'll ask at home. I hope that we are allowed to.'

'Me too!' said Anna. 'Well, 'bye – see you soon, I hope.' She ran off. By now the spectators were arriving, and the Ringmaster looked frantic. When he stalked past Sarah and Jack they heard him groan.

Anna had many last minute jobs to do

'They're late! They're late!' he kept muttering, and the children were very puzzled.

'Oh, we shall have to do without them,' groaned the poor Ringmaster.

What was wrong? Who was late? Just then the circus lorry with a covered-up cage on the back rolled slowly into the field. Whoever had been late had arrived! The Ringmaster strode up to the lorry, ordering the circus folk back. Waving his cane about he spoke angry words to the lorry driver who leant out of the window with a cigar in his mouth, and made some excuse for being late. A man sitting next to the driver, and dressed in a shiny blue circus costume, leapt out and explained something to the Ringmaster. Four tough circus men were given orders to uncover the cage. Everyone gasped as they gazed inside. Six beautiful tigers sat at the bars, showing massive white teeth as they snarled and growled. Their striped golden coats shone and their elegant tails swished from side to side as they pawed the bars, displaying their sharp claws. Jack stared with admiration at their magnificence, and Sarah watched with fear lurking in her heart. People were by now buying tickets and gazed in wonder at the six magnificent beasts. The Ringmaster's jolly face was beaming with pride as he disappeared, with relief at last, into the Big Top. Soon everyone was squeezed into the big tent, and the band began to play.

'Come on, Sarah,' said Jack, as they stood outside in the field which was now almost empty of people.

Sarah grinned with a sigh of happiness. 'Oh, it will be wonderful tomorrow.'

They walked away. Everywhere was quiet, with occasional interludes of faint clapping and band music coming from the tent.

Mrs Thomas did not hesitate in her answer to Sarah about the next day, although she knew her husband would disapprove.

'So you've been asked out to the circus. How nice, dear. Of course you must go. How lovely to be invited to supper by a circus girl. It will be an exciting experience. I hope you have a good time.'

'Thank you, Mrs Thomas,' said Sarah gladly. 'I'm so pleased that it's convenient. I will tell Jack at school tomorrow.'

However Jack's parents were not too sure about letting Jack stay for a meal with Anna. They had never seen Anna and did not want their son to get into bad company.

'But I should think it will be all right,' Mr Wilton told Jack. 'You can go, but make sure you take good care of yourself.'

Jack nodded, though he could see that his mother didn't approve of the affair.

Now when Molly, Billy and Mark heard that Sarah was going to the circus they were furious. Mr Thomas refused to let his family go because of the noise the circus folk made outside his window, so that the Thomas children were extremely jealous of Sarah and played spiteful tricks on her. They poured water on her bedroom carpet and hid her schoolbooks. Billy daringly dropped a beetle into her slipper, but it soon crawled out. That evening Molly thought of another prank which was really quite a funny one if you look at it from Molly's side. Quite recently Mrs Thomas had thrown a number of rotten pears into the dustbin. Her children retrieved these, folded Sarah's sheets to make an apple-pie bed, and filled the bed with the rotten fruit. When the unfortunate girl climbed into bed there was a ripping of sheets and a revolting squelching noise! Sarah realized that it must be another rotten trick again.

After school on Tuesday, Molly watched enviously from the window at the back of her house as Mr and Mrs Wilton, Yvonne, Jack and Sarah entered the tent with music playing and happy faces all round. Because Mr Wilton had booked tickets in advance, they were in the front row with a superb view of everything. When Mr and Mrs Wilton had bought programmes from Anna and seen what a nice girl she was, they were very much in favour of Jack dining in her caravan. It was thrilling to see the performances of Lianio, Celia, Sasha and all the other folk and animals they had met. All the time while the circus show was going on, the Thomas children tried not to listen to the applause, music and laughter coming from outside their back door. How they wished that they were there! But Molly had a secret from all the rest of her family. Her friend, Caroline Potter, had invited her to the circus on Wednesday afternoon.

'Oh, of course I'll come, Caroline,' replied Molly,

though she knew that her mother, and especially her father, would forbid it. But she did not tell her parents and planned to slip away and visit the circus secretly.

Meanwhile, while Molly was thinking about this at home, Anna was leading Jack and Sarah away from the crowds swarming out of the Big Top. In a few moments their footsteps sounded on the rickety wooden steps leading up to a narrow door. Sarah was very excited. She had never been in any sort of caravan before, and this particular one looked very attractive, painted in thick green and black bands, with large red wheels and with white curtains at the windows. Inside, it was very neat, with one bunk bed and a bed which slid out from a sofa. There was an oil-lamp, and a sink fitted into one corner. Of course it had no taps, but there was a bucket underneath to collect water. It was just like a real house, with all the rooms fitted into one. Supper, fried fish and bread, was laid out on a square table by the window. There was a blue and white checked table-cloth. Jack and Sarah sat on stools at the table while Anna crouched near the open door next to the steps and boiled water for some tea in a rusty old kettle over a flickering fire on the ground outside. They drank from big white mugs and had a slice of pie for pudding containing some wild strawberries, which Anna had picked herself.

'We don't usually have pudding,' said Anna. 'But when we have visitors, Ma or I usually make some sort of pie if there is any filling for it.'

'It's all so different in a circus,' Sarah remarked,

as she looked through the window at some poodles being taken for a walk. 'Tell us about what you do. I don't suppose you go to school.'

'Yes we do.' Anna put down her mug of tea. 'There's a special big caravan where we circus children go each morning. The caravan is divided into two parts, one for seniors and one for juniors. Next year I'll be moving into the seniors. They have a proper trained teacher, but we juniors are taught by circus folk. My teacher is Jane Roland, the poodle trainer. We use slates for writing on. Yes, I know they're old-fashioned, but you can use them again and again so that you don't have to buy tons of expensive paper and new pencils and rubbers all the time. If we stay anywhere for a season or more, the eldest children have to go to a local school. But in the afternoons we learn circus tricks.'

'Ooh, what kind of things?' said Jack.

'It depends on what you are going to be when you grow up. If you are going to be a clown, you must be taught by a real clown to do funny things like falling over without hurting yourself. If you want to work with animals, you learn how to handle and treat them.'

'What are you going to be?' asked Jack.

'A sealion trainer,' replied Anna at once. 'I'm allowed to work with Mandy May's sealions, but I'd love one of my own. My Pa is Bernardo Banatta, the trapeze artist. Did you like his act today?'

'Smashing!'

'He's thrilling.'

'Thanks!' Anna was evidently pleased. 'I told you

Anna boiled water for some tea

about my Ma making costumes, didn't I? She's an excellent seamstress.'

The time went too quickly for Sarah and Jack. Before they knew it the sky was darkening and it was time to go home.

'Goodbye and thank you for a glorious time,' they said.

Sarah skipped back to the Thomases' house happily. She had made two new kindly friends and what a lovely day they had given her.

chapter four

The old barge

By now, the summer holidays were approaching, and Rockfield School was due to break up on the following Friday. On the Wednesday, however, Molly went off to the circus with Caroline. No one missed her for a while, until Mrs Thomas found her bedroom empty when she carried up some of Molly's clothes newly washed. Soon it was discovered that Molly had vanished, and the news didn't put Mr Thomas in a very good mood when he came home from work.

'Well, hasn't anyone seen her?' he boomed.

'Not since she came in after school,' replied his worried wife. 'She went upstairs and I thought she was there all the time. She – she must have – slipped out.'

'Oh, you stupid, careless woman!' cried Mr Thomas. 'Can't you look after your own children?'

It was around seven o'clock when Molly crept in at the back door. The circus had gone on longer than she had expected, and she had missed supper. Oh well, she would explain to her parents with some lie. Molly had thoroughly enjoyed the circus, and her stomach was full of ice cream. Suddenly a cold, stunning voice said, 'And WHERE do you think you've been?'

Molly stopped abruptly and faced her angry mother. 'I – I've been – er ... er ...'

'Come and explain to your father at once!'

Molly trudged into the living-room, thinking up a dishonest excuse as she went.

'Well?' said her father as she stood before him.

'I went to Caroline's house for supper. I told Mum – she must have forgotten.'

Mr Thomas' fierce eyes were fixed on his wife.

'What nonsense and lies!' exclaimed Mrs Thomas. 'She hasn't mentioned it to me.'

'Well, you ought to have found out. It's too bad, Fiona! You're so thoughtless and irresponsible! I think you should at least know what your own children are doing. I shouldn't be surprised if Molly *did* tell you! You know what a bad memory you've got.'

'Molly, will you go upstairs and get ready for bed?' said Mrs Thomas, meaning to speak privately to her husband.

'What, already?' cried Molly, but her father's frown sent her to the door. Just then Sarah came in and bumped into Molly, who growled, 'Clumsy fool!'

'Could you two run upstairs, please?' said Mrs Thomas. When they had gone she lifted something off the floor. It had dropped from Molly's pocket when the two girls collided. Molly was unaware that the crumpled paper was now in her mother's hand. Mrs Thomas looked furious as she read the words on Molly's paper.

50

'What's that? Give it to me!' ordered Mr Thomas, observing his wife's angry countenance. His face clouded over as he ran his eyes over the fancy print. It was a crumpled programme from the circus.

'MOLLY!' yelled Mrs Thomas.

Molly tried to make excuses but it was no good. Her mother had distinctly seen the paper flutter from her pocket. Mr Thomas defended his daughter and called for Sarah, insisting that it was all her fault. 'If you'd never gone to that circus with those Wiltons, it would never have happened. MY Molly would never have dreamed of going after I'd forbidden it. My Molly is a good girl, but you're a bad influence on her – you made her go against my orders. I will not have it! Make sure that you keep away from Molly. You're a bad influence on my children – it would have been better if you'd never come here!'

Sarah's eyes brimmed with tears.

'ALFRED! I shall not have this!' cried Mrs Thomas. 'How can you say such things! How dare you insult poor Sarah! It is ...'

The row went on for ages, and Sarah wept as she sank back into bed after the nastiest day she had had with the Thomases. Mr Thomas and his children seemed to get worse each day. Sarah had never met such horrid people before. However, next morning something rather nice arrived. It was the promised letter from her mother, and it cheered her up a lot. It was a lovely long one, telling of everything going on in Canada. Mrs Parkinson said that Aunt Harriet was recovering very slowly and Sarah's mother might be home within a fortnight, if all went well.

Friday came at last, and at three o'clock the children were let out of school, chanting,

'No more school today,
No more school tomorrow
No more days of boring work
And no more days of sorrow!'

Everyone was happy. Boys and girls rambled arm-in-arm through the streets, laughing loudly and swinging satchels. The teachers, glad of a rest, drove off in their cars, and parents greeted the youngest of the children. Shouts of joy filled the air as pupils danced home under the hot summer sun. Sarah skipped merrily along the pavement. She was sure that, with Jack and Anna, she would thoroughly enjoy the holiday. Just then, Molly and Mark came running by, happily tearing up their old school jotters and filling the gutter with bits of paper that had untidy writing scribbled all over them. Shouting and shoving, the two Thomas children raced home.

On the first Tuesday afternoon of the holidays, Anna took Jack and Sarah somewhere they had never been before. They walked right to the end of the circus field, where trees grew close together. Weeping willows drooped their boughs, and oak trees bore many leaves. Little flowers peeped through the green blades of grass, and bees hummed busily about them. The children came to a grassy slope with uneven stone steps leading down to a river. The water was clear, with ripples running over it and a swiftly flowing current. Little waves turned to foam as they rushed over rocks which stuck out above the water's surface. Fishes darted here and there, but could only be recognized as black shadows. A tiny frog was basking in the sun on a rock. Thrushes chirped; blackbirds hopped about among the branches of the trees, whistling merry tunes; there was even a kingfisher perched on a bush, eyeing fishes under the water. Without warning, he suddenly darted beneath the surface and came up with a silver fish wriggling about in his beak. Pleased with his catch, the kingfisher strutted along a branch, with his smooth orange breast sticking out and his blue wings folded behind his back. The children kept quite still, so as not to disturb the creatures, but Jack could not help coughing. Spreading his wings, the kingfisher darted away. The birds in the trees chirped out a warning, fishes disappeared behind rocks, and frogs jumped into the water.

'It's lovely!' exclaimed Sarah. 'I've never been here before. To tell you the truth, I'd never been in the fields before the circus came.'

'I come here to wash and bathe,' said Anna. 'But this isn't all. Look further down the river!'

'It's a boat,' exclaimed Jack, peering at the object in the distance.

'A barge,' Anna told him. 'Come on!'

They walked along the river bank, treading only on the grass and avoiding the pretty flowers. The long green blades of grass came up further than

53

their ankles. As they got nearer, they could see that it was a barge moored to a post on the river-bank and needing a new coat of its blue and yellow paint. The name showed faintly round the prow of the boat.

'GLIDING PRINCESS,' read Sarah, screwing up her forehead. 'It's hard to make out the letters.'

'This barge isn't used any more – it's on display,' explained Anna. 'I think you're allowed on board.'

At once Sarah and Jack clambered on to the deck and made their way to the cabin.

'Oh!' exclaimed Sarah, as she looked through one of its windows. 'Come and see!'

Jack peered through the other window, and Anna opened the door and went in. There was a bunk bed, and a table of rotting wood with an old beer mug on top. There were two stools with padded seats, an old broken oil-lamp rested on a bench, and moth-eaten curtains hung at the windows. Jack and Sarah followed Anna into the cabin.

'Look at this!' said Jack in a disgusted voice, holding up the edge of a blanket on the bunk bed Sarah shivered as a spider fell off it on to the floor. The blanket was faded, and had been patched up in the middle where a hole had been torn.

'At least somebody's mended it,' said Sarah.

'And the beds have been made.'

'And the windows have been cleaned.'

'Well, it's not much good having a barge on display if it's never looked after. I suppose someone comes here each month to tidy it up.'

'The walls are musty, though.'

As they got nearer, they could see it was a barge

'Anna, why do they keep the broken oil-lamp and beer mug?'

'Probably so that folks can see what it used to be like. This is a river barge. The very old-fashioned ones were pulled by horses walking on a towpath. This one has got an engine, though.'

Jack went outside the cabin to take a look.

'You know what I'm going to do?' said Anna to Sarah, thoughtfully.

'What?'

'I'm going to ask my Ma to give me some sandwiches we can eat here.'

'Oh, that would be nice!'

'I wish I could sleep here!'

Sarah looked doubtfully at the musty walls and uninviting beds.

Anna grinned at her. 'I'd bring my own clean blankets and sheets, of course,' she assured Sarah.

Just then Jack sauntered back into the cabin.

'Quite a nice engine,' he said. 'I'm pretty sure it's broken, though.'

'Jack, Anna's going to ask her Ma to give us a picnic to have here,' said Sarah.

'It'll need to be about half past three,' remarked Anna. 'How about tomorrow?'

'That will be fine,' replied Jack. 'It's a pity you haven't got summer holidays like us!'

Eventually they went out of the cabin, and saw a thrush perching on the edge of the barge. He flew away as soon as his beady eyes caught sight of the children. The three friends went up the stone steps and into the circus field, and parted after arranging to meet there in the afternoon of the following day.

When Sarah entered the Thomases' house, the telephone rang. Mrs Thomas picked up the receiver. Sarah heard a short conversation.

'Oh, hello, Mrs Wilton,' said Mrs Thomas. 'Yes, I've heard that Jack and Sarah are friends ... Of course, it's not rude to ask ... Actually, she hasn't much to do here. It'll be lovely for her ... Tomorrow evening? Yes, that will be fine. What time? ... Eight o'clock? Yes, that's quite all right ... Goodbye, then.'

Mrs Thomas put back the telephone receiver and, turning to Sarah, said, 'Well, well, you've been invited to stay with Jack overnight.'

'Oh, how lovely!' cried Sarah. 'I hope you don't mind me going when I'm supposed to be staying with you.'

'Of course not,' replied Mrs Thomas.

The next afternoon, Sarah and Jack met Anna in the circus field as arranged. Anna was carrying a bag containing sandwiches and a carton of milk. It was extremely shady by the river, and the scent of flowers filled the air. The birds sang cheerfully, and the kingfisher was doing his usual spot of fishing. Butterflies, white or orange and black, fluttered about resting on the flowers. The children walked down the river-bank to the barge. Some moorhens were swimming along in the water, and a blackbird, who was sitting on the cabin roof, flew away when he caught sight of the children boarding the barge. Inside the cabin, the three friends made it as cosy as possible. They set out the sandwiches on the table,

57

and even poured some milk into the old beer mug.

'Ugh! I'm not drinking out of that! It's years old!' said Jack, drawing the curtains back as far as they would go to let in some more sunlight. Soon they were all tucking into sausage sandwiches, and drinking milk from paper cups.

'Anna, I dare you to drink out of that old beer mug,' said Sarah.

Anna picked it up and sniffed. 'It smells funny,' she said, and put the mug to her lips, taking ever such a tiny sip.

'Well?' said Jack.

'There's nothing wrong with it,' replied Anna, and gulped the rest of the milk in the mug.

'Oh, look!' said the shocked Sarah suddenly. 'Someone else has been here since yesterday. They've thrown an empty beer-can on the floor.'

Jack laughed as he picked up the can. 'You sound as if no one else is allowed here,' he said. 'Anyone can come. It's a public place. The barge is on display. It's not good to drop litter though.'

'Let's find a shallow place in the river and paddle,' said Anna suddenly.

'Oh, what a good idea,' said Sarah.

They cleared away the remains of the sandwiches and put the paper cups into Anna's bag. As the girls were climbing off the barge, something in the stern caught Jack's attention.

'Oh, look!' he exclaimed. 'What's happened to the engine? It looks brand new!'

'Well, someone must have cleaned and polished

it. There's nothing wrong in that, is there?' said Anna, climbing on to the bank.

'I didn't say there was,' remarked Jack, as he got off the boat too. Soon they found a shallow place in the river to paddle. As they dipped their bare feet in the cool water, fishes scattered in all directions.

'I've got one,' cried Jack suddenly.

'What?' said Anna. She and Sarah turned to see a silver fish slithering about in Jack's cupped hands.

'Ooh!' said Sarah. 'Put it back or it will die!'

Lowering his hands into the water, Jack let the fish go, and it swam off as fast as an arrow from a bow.

'I scooped it up in my hands,' said Jack proudly, wiping his wet fingers on his shorts.

While they were all paddling in the shallow water, Jack slipped on a slimy rock, and fell aside on to the bank, knocking Anna's shoe into the river.

'Oh, Jack!' squealed Anna. 'My shoe!'

The shoe floated down the river in the swiftly flowing current. The kingfisher, perching on a branch nearby, wondered what kind of fish it was. Maybe a sole! Anna waded further into the river, until she had water up to her knees and her skirt was trailing in it.

'Oh, I can't reach it,' she wailed.

'Look!' cried Sarah. 'It's floating towards the barge.'

At once Jack ran to the boat, and, climbing on board, looked over the side. There was the shoe being carried along by the current. Jack stretched his arm into the water and rescued Anna's shoe. He carried it back to Anna with water dripping on to the grass and drops coming from a hole in the heel. Anna pulled a face as she waded to the bank and squeezed water out of the shoe which Jack gave her, apologizing for the incident. Anna fetched a purple towel from her caravan so that they could all dry their feet. Then, as the circus girl had some money, they all went to the sweetshop.

On their way, as they passed the Thomases' house, they saw two boys rolling about on the pavement. Grit was flying in their eyes and they were tugging at one another's hair as they yelled and screeched. Fists lashed out and legs kicked viciously. Sarah recognized the boys – Mark and his friend Jeremy. Friend? Did I say 'friend'? Why, they looked like great foes! Something was rolling about between them. It was a bag of sweets. The boys shouted at one another as they fought.

'They're MINE!' screeched Jeremy.

'You said you would!'

'I won't!'

'You must! You said you'd give me half! Oooch! That hurt!'

'I said *some*, not 'alf. Ger off me!'

Mark snatched the bag of sweets which was causing the trouble. He yelled in pain as Jeremy kicked his leg hard, and the bag of sweets flew on to the road, where the contents spilt and were squashed by a car which suddenly whizzed past. Still Jeremy and Mark fought. A surprised old lady peered through her window, wondering what on earth was going on.

Fists lashed out and legs kicked viciously

Suddenly Jack rushed over to the fighting pair and hauled Jeremy off Mark who was shouting while he kicked and punched Jeremy and bit him with his sharp teeth.

'Leave me alone!' Jeremy screamed at Jack, struggling to get away and to have his revenge on Mark for punching his nose and making it bleed. Anna pulled Mark from the ground, and held him away from Jeremy, who was spitting, cursing, and swinging his arms wildly to get free and strike Mark. The latter lashed out at Jeremy, but Anna pulled him back so that he couldn't reach.

'Look, it's no use fighting over those sweets,' said Jack sternly. 'They've fallen on to the road and have been run over by a car.'

The boys began to calm down, and, panting after their desperate struggle, stared fiercely at one another. Suddenly Mark gave a yell which sounded like a warcry. 'Lemme go!' he shouted.

As they were next to the Thomases' house, Sarah opened the garden gate, and Anna shoved Mark through. Jeremy was pushed by Jack down the street. Gritting his teeth and scowling, Mark strutted up the garden path and rang the doorbell ferociously. After a rough push, the infuriated Jeremy sauntered down the street with his hands in his pockets, kicking a stone along the pavement and pouting.

Before they parted, Sarah told Jack she would come along to his house about eight o'clock. Mr Thomas had been pleased to hear that Sarah would be leaving for a time. 'I'll be glad to be rid of the nuisance,' he had said.

Sarah lost no time in packing her case, putting in her nightdress, a toothbrush and plastic tumbler, a sponge, her dressing-gown and her best blue dress. Then she went down to supper.

chapter five

Unexpected events

Mr Thomas had come home in a very bad mood after a day at work when everything had seemed to go wrong. Sarah could tell by the way he slammed doors and spoke gruffly that she ought to avoid him. At supper time he said to Sarah, 'So you're going away, are you? Well, there's no need to hurry back here. Stay as long as they'll have you. I've seen you chatting to those dirty gypsies again. If you want my advice, keep away from that circus. If you were my daughter, I'd never let you go near those folk. But of course you don't care what I think.'

'Oh, Alfred! Leave her alone!' said his wife.

'I don't want Sarah to come back,' cried Molly. 'I hate her.'

'Be quiet!' ordered Mrs Thomas. 'I won't stand for such nonsense.'

After supper Sarah came into the sitting-room to say goodbye to the Thomases. 'As I've said before,' growled Mr Thomas, 'stay away as long as you can. Don't hurry back. I won't miss you. Neither will the kids.'

'No, we won't miss you,' agreed Billy. 'Don't come back.' He broke into a chant. 'Don't come back, don't come back, don't come—'

'Shut up!' commanded Mrs Thomas. She took Sarah to one side and spoke to her in a low voice. 'Don't listen to them. They don't mean it, of course. Forget what they said. Now here's your suitcase. I hope you have a lovely time, dear. The Wiltons are such nice people. Now just enjoy yourself and forgive my husband and children. They don't know any better. Just forget what they said.'

'That's all very well,' thought Sarah as she left through the front door. 'But it's hard not to take any notice of those nasty words. I'm sick of Mr Thomas and his children.'

She strode along to Jack's house and as she walked she almost bumped into someone. It was Jack.

'Oh, hello!' grinned Sarah. But Jack looked glum. He flicked a lock of glossy hair away from his eyes. 'I've got bad news.'

'Oh! What's wrong?'

'Some friends of my mother are travelling to Wales and have just dropped in at our house. Mother hasn't seen them for nine years, so she feels she ought to put them up for the night. There are three of them altogether and we have only one spare room. That's why mother asked me to come and ask you if you would mind coming another time instead. We're very sorry, but you do understand, don't you?'

'Yes.' Sarah looked forlorn. 'But surely three people can't all sleep in one spare room?'

'I know. I expect one will use *my* bedroom. That means I'll have to sleep in Yvonne's room on that beastly camp bed that keeps breaking.'

'Poor you! I – I guess I'd better go – go back to the Thomases' house, then.'

Jack was sad to see that Sarah was so disappointed. 'Look, Sarah, I'm awfully sorry about it but it can't be helped, and—'

'It's not that, Jack. I don't mind coming another time. But, you see – well, I know I sound a coward, but I'm scared to go back to Mr Thomas. His children will jeer at me and he will groan – and – and he was in *such* a bad mood when I left. You don't know what he is like in a temper. He shouts and bawls and orders people about and – and he's an awful man. I just couldn't face going back right now. You see, if I'd come to your house tonight, he would have been in a better mood when I got back.'

'I understand,' said the sympathetic Jack. 'I had an Uncle George like that. But he was very old and died. I can't say I was sorry.'

Sarah sniffed. 'I'll – I'll be off then. Oh, dear! I'm so frightened.'

'Don't go,' said Jack. 'Perhaps Anna will have you and you can stay overnight with her.'

'I can't just invite myself,' argued Sarah.

'Well – well, come on anyway.'

They made their way towards the fields. The sun was getting low in the sky and the circus folk were frying their evening meal over fires which crackled outside the wagons. Delicious smells of fried eggs, sausages and bacon filled the air. The animals were satisfying their appetites as well, and noisily consumed their own various foods. A man sitting on the steps of a wagon played a quiet tune on his banjo.

66

In the distance, the river water could be heard flowing swiftly.

Jack strode over to Anna's Ma, who was outside her caravan sewing some frills round the bodice of a lace frock. The woman looked up as he asked politely, 'Please could you tell me where Anna is?'

Her Ma pointed a bony finger in the direction of the river.

Sarah and Jack trotted hastily to the uneven stone steps and went down. Anna was sitting with her back against a tree, carelessly throwing stones into the water where they fell with a quiet 'plop'. Hearing the footsteps of Jack and Sarah, she looked round and grinned. 'Hullo,' she said.

'Hello,' said Jack. He went over to her and explained the situation. 'So have you any idea where Sarah can stay?' he ended by enquiring.

Anna smiled and, with a grubby hand, pushed a lock of greasy black hair away from her somewhat dirt-streaked face. 'S'pose you want to stay with me?' she said. ' 'Fraid you can't, 'cos I've no room in my wagon. Now, if we'd a caravan as big as Lianio's, you could – he's got two bunks 'cos his chimps go in as well.'

'Oh,' said Jack in disappointment.

Anna brightened up suddenly. 'I KNOW!' she cried.

'What?' said Jack. 'And there's no need to shout.'

'Oh, it's a fabulous idea!' cried the excited Anna, bobbing up and down in glee. 'The barge! We'll all sleep on the barge!'

Jack looked doubtful, and turning to Sarah asked, 'What do you think?'

'Mrs Thomas might not approve and Mr Thomas definitely won't,' replied Sarah, who was not too keen on the idea.

But Anna was already making arrangements. 'The Thomases needn't know,' she said. 'They think you're staying the night with Jack, and you *are* – but only on the barge.'

'I expect mother would let me sleep there as we're short of beds,' Jack said.

'Are you sure?' Anna was doubtful. 'If you mention the barge she might not let you go. You'd better just ask if you can stay overnight with Sarah, but don't say where. Some grown-ups can't understand there's nothing wrong with things like sleeping on a barge.'

'You're probably right,' said Jack uneasily.

As Anna began to fill in details the whole thing seemed rather exciting. 'Jack, you and I must fetch night-clothes, and we'll all wash in the river. I'll get clean sheets, blankets and pillows, of course. Sarah and I will sleep in the top bunk, and Jack down below.'

Jack and Sarah began to add their own ideas. 'Someone can bring a torch,' suggested Sarah. 'Who's got one? I haven't.'

'I haven't either,' said Anna.

'Nor me,' said Jack, 'but my father has one which I could borrow. I say, we could have something to eat before we go to sleep.'

'Yes,' agreed the others.

'The barge! We'll all sleep on the barge!'

'It will be great fun on the barge,' remarked Sarah.

'You see,' grinned Anna, 'my idea wasn't so bad after all, was it? Let's go an' get some blankets an' stuff from my caravan.'

They all went up the stone steps and across the circus field. They met Lianio carrying a bucket of water to his caravan. The children stopped to chat while the man sat down on the steps of his wagon and lowered the bucket of water to the ground. Sarah liked Lianio very much and enjoyed looking at his twinkling blue eyes, smiling lips, smooth face and his mop of glossy brown hair.

'Hello,' said Jack. 'How are Gepetto and Jessica?'

'Hello,' replied Lianio, rolling up his shirt-sleeves to reveal sun-tanned, hairy arms. He dipped his arms into the bucket and splashed fresh water over his face, clearing it of dirt-stains. 'The chimps are fine. I'm getting ready to take them to an extra show.'

'We'd better not hold you up, then,' said Anna, who was eager to get on with preparations for the night. 'We've some work to do, as well. Come on, you two.'

Jack was sorry to leave Lianio because he had been hoping to see the chimpanzees.

Anna took them to her caravan and opened the door. No one else was there, so she beckoned Sarah and Jack inside. The circus girl gathered together some sheets, blankets and biscuits. 'Jack!' she said. 'You bring my pillows and that rug. Sarah, you'll find some choc'late in the cupboard. Bring a few books from that shelf too, and chuck your case on the bunk. You c'n come back for it.'

The three children left the caravan, and set off across the field laden with various articles. Down by the river, the animals and birds had retired to rest. Flowers had closed their petals, and their pretty heads were nodding. Soon the children were on board the *Gliding Princess*, and hurried into the cabin. Everything was made ready. The mouldy blankets, sheets and pillows were dragged off the bunk, and clean ones were laid down. Biscuits and chocolate were piled on the table, and books were arranged on the bench.

'We'll go back and collect our night things now,' said Anna. 'Jack, you'll need to arrange things at home. Remember that torch!'

They all left the barge, and parted at Anna's caravan, where Jack set off home deep in thought. Anna and Sarah went back into the caravan, where Anna took a plain, orange nightdress out of a drawer and an empty pail containing a sponge from under the washbasin.

'Now have we forgotten anything?' she asked.

'Well, you haven't got a toothbrush,' said Sarah.

'Oh, I don't need to bother with that,' said Anna, and nodded at the bunk bed. 'Don't forget your suitcase! Got it? Right! Come on, then!'

They opened the caravan door just as Anna's Ma was entering.

'What's the meaning of this?' she enquired,

eyeing their burdens. 'Where are you off to?'

'I'm going to sleep on the barge tonight, Ma,' replied Anna.

The woman nodded, and went into her caravan.

Jack took quite a time coming. He found his mother busy in the kitchen preparing a late supper for the visitors. She was perplexed and frustrated because beds and meals had all to be made ready in a rush.

'Mother?' said Jack cautiously. He knew he would have to wriggle round her to get her to say 'yes'. 'You know how we're short of beds?'

'Mmm.' She was busy chopping up carrots as fast as a machine.

'Well, I arranged to stay with Sarah overnight. Is that all right? You see, now we won't have all that trouble with camp beds, and I'll be out of your way as you are so very busy.'

Mrs Wilton was touched by these last few words. 'Well, I suppose so.'

'I'll be back for breakfast. Are – are you sure you don't mind me going away for the night?'

'Dash it! I've cut my finger. What? Oh – yes, yes! Go and stay with Sarah.'

Jack hugged her. 'Thanks, mother. Shall I fetch you a plaster?'

'There's no time, dear. Now run along and pack some things. Yes, it will be a little easier about the beds now.'

Jack felt rather glad that his father had gone to a meeting that evening because if Mr Wilton had been at home he might not have given his permission. After collecting the torch and his night things, and changing into long trousers as the evening was turning chilly, he kissed Mrs Wilton goodbye and left. As he did so, he wondered if it was wrong to do a thing like this. Of course not! It was a help for his mother not to have him there just then. There was nothing wrong in sleeping on the barge anyway. He was old enough to look after himself, and the girls needed to be taken care of. In this way, Jack managed to assure himself that he was doing the right thing. But he felt doubtful as he crossed the circus field.

All three children were soon walking along the river-bank towards the barge. She rocked gently on the rippled water, and the setting sun made her look a pretty picture. There was a clatter of feet as the children got on to the deck. With squeals of delight, they ran into the cabin and dropped their burdens. It was rather dark, so they drew the curtains, and switched on the torch, which made strange shadows on the musty walls. Jack beamed and said, 'Good torch, eh? My father's. I had to take it from the drawer in his room.'

'Those biscuits look tasty,' said Sarah, eyeing them.

'Well, we'll wash first before it's too dark to see,' Anna said, picking up her pail and sponge. Sarah opened her case and unpacked the articles she needed. Then she joined Jack and Anna by the river. Anna filled her pail, and, dipping in her sponge, began to wash. Jack produced a bar of pink soap, and soon all three were clean. They went back to the barge, and, in the cabin, switched on the torch. Then they all put on night-clothes.

'Posh, aren't you?' said Anna, staring enviously at Sarah's pink nightdress, adorned with frills and lace. Her own was very plain. Jack looked at his watch.

'What does your watch say?' asked Anna.

'Tick, tick,' replied Jack.

Sarah laughed. Anna gave Jack a friendly punch, and grinned.

'It's long past bedtime,' said Sarah, looking at her own watch. 'Let's read in bed for a quarter of an hour.'

'And eat,' added Anna, picking up the chocolate and biscuits. 'Bags sleep in the top bunk with Sarah.'

The two girls climbed under warm blankets, while Jack got under a comfortable rug below and rested his head on the pillow. Biscuits and chocolate were shared out, and eaten while the children read books. Anna read about sealions, of course.

After a quarter of an hour, the books were put away, and all the food had been consumed. Sarah filled her tumbler with water, which she used to clean her teeth. She switched off the torch and, as they were all tired, they were soon fast asleep.

Late at night, Sarah was awoken by a loud noise. Before they had gone to sleep, Jack had pulled rusty bolts across the cabin door. Now someone was shaking the door from the other side, and a muffled voice was saying, 'Damn this door – it's locked.'

'Well, who locked it?' asked another strange voice.

'How should I know?'

'It must be jammed.'

Someone shook the door violently. 'Course it's not jammed – it's bolted from the inside. There must be a tramp or someone inside. Come on, help me with the door! We'll have to break it down.'

Sarah was horrified. Who was at the door in the night? Who so badly wanted to get into the cabin? Vandals, perhaps. But no – she could now recognize another noise which had been droning in the background since she had been awakened – the purring of an engine! The boat must be in motion!

The frightened girl shook Anna, whispering quickly, 'Wake up, Anna, wake up!'

Anna rolled to the side, giving a grunt, and without opening her eyes asked sleepily, 'What is it?'

'Someone's trying to get in,' said Sarah in a scared voice. 'Someone's breaking the door down!'

Anna heard banging, and sat up, alarmed. 'Hide!' she said. 'Where's the torch?'

'Jack's got it. Jack, wake up!'

Jack stirred, then, hearing the noise, sat up in surprise. 'What the heck's going on?' he said.

'Shh!' hissed Sarah, and quickly explained the situation. Jack grabbed his torch and dived under the bed, followed by the two frantic girls. Sarah's foot disappeared under the bunk just as the door crashed to the floor. Splinters of wood flew about, and twisted metal, amidst planks of split wood, lay on the floor. Heavy footsteps were heard as two people entered. In the light from the men's torches, the children saw a pair of big, black, laced boots stepping over the mess of splintered wood. These were followed by a pair of legs wearing baggy brown trousers, grey knitted socks, and dull brown shoes.

'Let's get out!' whispered Jack.

As they crept through the gap where a door had once been, they heard the noise of the engine more distinctly. When on the deck, the children could see in the moonlight the barge gliding slowly and placidly through the water.

'Hide!' hissed Anna.

Nearby was a huge box, on which was printed in bold black letters 'GROCERIES'. The three went to the box and crouched behind it. They had not been seen. It was most puzzling. Who had broken into the cabin? Who had put a box of groceries on to the barge? And then the children saw something even more puzzling. Lolloping about on the deck was a chimpanzee, in a white T-shirt and blue shorts. It was Gepetto! What on earth was he doing on board the barge?

'Don't tell me that Lianio is one of those men!' said Jack quietly.

'Oh no, he's far too nice!' Sarah assured him. 'Gepetto must have been stolen.'

'And I think I know who the thief is,' said Anna.

'Who?' whispered Jack's excited voice.

'Well, Lianio and Mr Jimminy were asked to travel to a fair a few miles away to give a performance with their animals,' Anna explained. 'As a large sum of money was offered in payment, Mr

Morgan let them go this evening around nine o'clock. Now I reckon that poor Lianio was knocked out on the journey by Mr Jimminy, who stole the chimp and brought him here. I never liked Mr Jimminy.'

'I think you must be right. I don't like Mr—' Jack stopped as one of the men appeared at the cabin door and scratched his head, ruffling his black, frizzled hair. He was not Mr Jimminy.

'I don't understand 'ow the door got locked from the inside if there's no one 'ere,' he said.

The children trembled when they heard the other man inside the cabin reply, 'Well, someone *has* been here. There are new blankets an' stuff an' someone's been sleeping in the beds. There's books 'ere as well.'

The man at the door went back into the cabin and said, 'Whoever was 'ere left in an 'urry. Look at the way the sheets are thrown back.'

Just then Gepettó loped in and jumped on one man's shoulder, startling him.

'Oh, drat!' he said. 'Why did we 'ave to bring these chimps? Where's the other one? Up to some mischief, I'll be bound!'

'The animals are worth a lot of money, Alf. We can maybe sell them,' said the other man calmly.

Anna winked at Sarah.

'Thieves!' said Jack, gritting his teeth.

The man with the black, frizzled hair strode out of the cabin and walked round it, peering all over the barge. The children were terrified in case they were discovered. But the man didn't see them. He just sauntered back into the cabin, saying to his friend, 'Can't spot anyone. They must 'ave jumped off. Least we've got rid of 'em.'

'They were only kids anyway,' added the other man.

'What d'you mean?'

'Look, these are kids' books here.'

'So they are.'

There was a pause before one of the men said, 'This barge ain't goin' fast enough, Ted. Why 'aven't you bought a speedboat?'

'Money doesn't grow on trees. I don't get much at that circus. I'm glad to be leaving it. It's all right for you, though. Why don't *you* buy a speedboat? This is the best I could manage. Remember it was me wot mended that engine.'

Jack nudged the girls and whispered, 'I told you someone had done something to the engine!'

'But didn't you hear what he said about leaving the circus?' put in Anna. 'It *must* be Mr Jimminy.'

'I agree,' said Sarah. 'But haven't the men got queer voices? They sound funny somehow, don't they?'

'Yes, they do,' Jack replied.

Just then one man cried, 'Look out! We're getting too close to the bank. You'd better go and steer. I'll stay here and get some sleep.'

'OK. But look after those stupid chimps.'

The man with the black, frizzled hair strode out of the cabin and over to the stern. From where they were hiding, the children could look into the cabin

The man ... was peering all over the barge

through the shattered doorway. In the moonlight they saw the dark outline of a figure putting a clay pipe into his mouth with some difficulty. He muttered to himself, 'Drat these mouth-'oles! They're too small!'

This remark puzzled the children.

'What does he mean by that?' asked Sarah.

Jack shrugged.

'Jack!' exclaimed Sarah suddenly. 'One of the men is called Alf, isn't he?'

'Yes.'

'Well, Mr Thomas' Christian name is Alfred, and Alf is short for that. Mr Thomas is nasty. I think he is one of those men. It would be easy for him to get down to the barge, because the river is so near his house.'

'You may be right,' said Jack, 'but we've seen the man who's steering, and he isn't Mr Jimminy *or* Mr Thomas. It can't be the two of them.'

The girls looked glum, but Sarah brightened up and exclaimed, 'They might be wearing disguises.'

'They might,' agreed Jack. 'I'll go up to the cabin and see if I can spot any false eyebrows or anything. The one in the cabin's asleep – I can hear him snoring.'

'Oh no! The man who's steering will see you!' cried Sarah in alarm.

'Don't go!' hissed Anna.

'It's all right,' replied Jack, and crept away before the girls could stop him. As he peeped through the doorway, the moonlight shone on the sleeping man's face. The skin looked rubbery and the brown hair was straggly. But then Jack saw that it was only a wig which had slipped back while the man slept, revealing the edge of a rubber mask! So this was what the remark about mouth-holes meant, and it must be the masks which had made the men's voices so squeaky and distorted. All the bits of jigsaw fitted into place! The triumphant Jack crept back to the girls and told them. But someone saw him! It was Gepetto. The excited chimpanzee woke the man in the cabin by scampering over his still body and rushing outside, chattering loudly. Jessica followed. Both the apes were delighted to see Jack and ran after him to the children's hiding place.

'Get them chimps away from them watches!' cried the man at the stern, as Jessica and Gepetto dived behind the grocery box. His companion came running out of the cabin and grabbed the squealing Jessica. What a surprise he got! There were three children crouching behind the box in night-clothes!

chapter six

Over the sea

'Alf! Come here!' cried the astonished man. Jessica wriggled free and scampered away. Alf came quickly and was amazed to see the children.

'Told you someone 'ad been sleepin' 'ere,' he said gruffly. 'Trust these kids to be 'ere.'

The other man spat on the deck. 'Drat!' he said. 'What can we do? If we let them go they'll go to the coppers and tell 'em.'

Holding Jack's collar Alf pulled the boy to his feet. 'Put 'em in the cabin!' he growled.

The girls were also pulled to their feet and put with Jack. Alf went to stand by the engine while the other man made himself comfortable on one bed with all the blankets, the rug and the pillows. As there was only room for the girls on the other bed, Jack had to sleep on the hard wooden bench. None of the children had blankets, but it was warm enough to get to sleep without them.

When they woke it was about half past eight and the barge was not moving. The two men were seated by the table on stools and were discussing what to do with the children.

'I don't want 'em,' Alf was saying.

'But we've got to keep them.'

'Look, Ted, by the time they get to the coppers we'll be out of the country.'

'Not necessarily; they might get there too soon.'

'P'raps Pierre will 'ave 'em.'

'Probably he will. He's got a big house and likes children. When we've left France he can let them loose into the streets before he goes to Paris to set up his new jeweller's shop.'

The children were horrified. It seemed that they were to be taken to a house in France or something and someone called Pierre was going to shove them into the streets. Sarah began to cry.

'Oh, so you're awake, then,' said Alf, looking up. 'Ger out of bed. We're going on a journey. Got any decent clothes?'

They had, so they put them on, with Sarah sobbing and sniffing all the time. After this hurried change of attire the children watched miserably from the cabin doorway as Alf threw Sarah's case over the side of the barge into the river with the books and night-clothes weighing it down inside.

'Don't want any clues for the cops,' he said.

'You'll be sorry for this, you rogues!' Jack cried, plucking up his courage.

Alf pressed the boy's cheek with a clenched fist. 'Mind what you say, laddie,' he growled.

Just then Alf felt a sharp slap on his back. He swung round clenching his fists. There was Gepetto chattering excitedly. Alf bent down and said angrily, 'You villain! You little pest! How dare you?'

He received a sharp slap on the nose from the

cheeky chimpanzee. Anna giggled. Alf stood up-right, glaring. His fist lashed out and hit the bed post as Anna dodged.

'There's no need to make a fuss,' said Ted. 'Leave 'em alone. At this rate we won't be there till next week.'

Then the children were taken out on to the deck. It was a lovely day but they were in no mood to be cheerful. The barge was moored in a lonely spot where patches of dog-roses grew. A weeping willow drooped towards the ground and other trees with crisp dry bark grew all around. In the background were tangled bushes with prickly leaves and ferns growing amongst them. A crow, perched on a branch, cawed slowly and steadily. Ted and Alf went over to the big grocery box and opened the lid. The children did not know what to expect as the men pulled something out. There might be bags of potatoes, cabbages, jars of jam and packets of tea – or would it be all kinds of watches? Alf had told Ted to keep the chimpanzees away from watches when they had rushed to the box. What did come out was a big wooden crate, so the grocery box must only have been a disguise for it. Ted and Alf lifted the heavy object between them and using much effort carried it to the bank, calling the children to follow them. Jessica pawed at the crate, much to the annoyance of the two men.

'Get that crazy chimp away from these watches,' growled Alf. He tried to kick Jessica, but Jack pulled her away in time. Alf snarled. The two men laid down the crate while Ted cut the rope which

The men carried the crate towards the tangled bushes

moored the barge. Now the boat was loose and she floated down the river. The men lifted the crate and carried it towards the tangled bushes, trampling on the poor dog-roses. Meekly the children followed.

'Dash!' said Alf as he was scratched on the arm by a sharp twig.

'Ow!' exclaimed Ted as he was stung by a nettle.

'Here you kids, come an' 'elp.'

The children held the edges of the crate as it was carried in and out of the thick prickly bushes. At last the men put the crate down amongst some long twisted grass. Alf took a rusty steel key out of his trouser pocket and parted some bits of bush. Behind it was a dirty grey lock. Alf fitted the key into the lock and turned it. When he gave a rough push a whole part of bush swung inwards. There was really a gate behind the bush where no one could find it. The greenery disguised this opening. Everyone trooped in, including the chimpanzees who scampered ahead. Beyond the gate was a kind of lawn, about twenty metres square. Round it was a high wall hidden by bushes. In the middle stood – what do you think? It was a small bluish-grey helicopter with a single propeller.

'What do you think of 'er?' said Alf to Ted.

'She's a beauty,' replied the man.

'Well, let's load 'er.'

Alf opened the door in the helicopter and the two men shifted the crate inside.

'There's a nice supply of food in 'ere,' said Alf, patting the helicopter's side. He turned and scowled at the children saying, ''Ave we gotter bring 'em?

Why not leave 'em 'ere with the gate locked?'

Ted shook his head. 'Cops'll be looking for 'em,' he said. 'If they're found they'll tell.'

Alf spat on the ground.

Jessica and Gepetto had already hopped into the helicopter. How interesting it was! There were two seats, blankets and cushions, not to mention a large pile of tins containing appetizing fruits, fish and meat. Jessica dived at the tins and sent them flying higgledy-piggledy over the floor. Hearing a clatter the two men rushed into the helicopter. Alf tripped over a tin of pilchards which was rolling through the door. Ted grabbed Jessica and after giving her a spanking smacked Gepetto as well, because he did not know who had done it. Then he called to the children, 'Hey, you kids, get inside!'

Jack went in first, followed by the girls who were very unwilling. The men sat in the seats at the front opposite the controls.

'You can sit on those rugs in the back,' said Ted to the children. The youngsters all sank down on to the soft blankets and cushions. It was very hot in the back of the helicopter and all three were very miserable. There was a burring noise, as the propeller started to spin. Gradually the helicopter began to ascend. The children stared with blank faces at the crate which stood behind Alf's seat. They were worried. What would their parents think? Up in the air they would never be found! It was horrid being in a hot stuffy helicopter with two utterly horrible men. Sarah felt sick. She didn't like travelling. Jack knew that his parents would be awfully worried and upset. These men spoke of letting them loose in the streets. They would starve! They would die of hunger! Oh dear, and where were they going? Ted and Alf had mentioned France.

Anna knew that her Ma and Pa would be worried too. Whatever would they think?

Poor Sarah was the most upset of all. In a few days her mother might return to find that her daughter had been kidnapped. Why, oh why, had she decided to sleep on the barge?

Gepetto came and put his hairy arm round Sarah to comfort her although he didn't know what was wrong. Jessica gave Anna a tin of peaches from the disorderly pile but there was no tin-opener to remove the lid.

Up in the sky fluffy white clouds floated by. Alf, who was not piloting, gave a weary sigh, saying, 'I'm taking this mask off. It's all 'ot an' sticky and the mouth-'oles are too small. We'll soon be out of England so it'll be all right now. I can 'ardly breathe.'

The children looked up with interest. Was Alf Mr Thomas?

Carefully the man began to peel off his rubber mask. The first thing the children saw was a shaggy eyebrow, and then a mop of dark messy hair as a black, frizzled wig toppled off. A pair of shifty grey eyes looked out as the mask came down a little further. But when she saw the nose Sarah knew that Alf was not Mr Thomas. The latter had a long narrow nose but this one was large and fat with wide nostrils. Alf peeled off the rest of the mask. What a disappointment! Not one of the children had seen him before. The hefty Alf had a short, tufty, black beard and possessed a dark serious face with thick pink lips. Neither Jack, Sarah nor Anna liked the look of him at all.

'You not takin' yours off, Ted?' he said.

'Well, watch the controls then,' said Ted.

'I bet this one is Mr Jimminy,' whispered Anna.

Ted heard these words, laughed ironically, and remarked, 'You'll be surprised, lassie.'

Anna was puzzled. She was sure this was Mr Jimminy. The man tossed a light brown wig on to the floor revealing glossy brown hair. Anna's mouth dropped open, for Mr Jimminy had black hair! Who was it then? Five pairs of eyes (Jessica and Gepetto were looking) watched Ted as he ripped off half the rubber mask. The children and chimpanzees saw a smooth sun-tanned face, a slightly freckled nose, blue eyes, and when the other half of the mask was pulled off they saw – guess who! Lianio! The children were horrified. They had liked Lianio but he was a fraudulent, wicked man inside, though he had pretended to be friendly and kind.

Seeing his master's face revealed, Gepetto ran in delight to Lianio but got a hard kick. Jessica also tried to get to her master but was fended off.

'Ger off, you little pest!' snapped the man. 'Why don't you keep out of the way?'

The children recognized the voice of the chimpanzee trainer now that the tight mask which had distorted it had been removed. All three of them were disgusted with Lianio. They sat with their backs to him and wouldn't say a word. Anna bit her nails, Jack kept looking at his watch and Sarah sat feeling hungry for some breakfast, though it didn't look as if they were going to have any.

Meanwhile, back home, Jack's mother was rather perturbed. It was well after breakfast time, when her son had promised to return. Her three friends had left in their car a little while ago. Where was Jack? What was he doing? Now she wished she had found out more details on the previous evening, but she had been very busy and frustrated with so much on her hands. Eventually she decided to phone up Mrs Thomas, who was washing the breakfast dishes when the telephone rang. She lifted the receiver to hear Mrs Wilton's urgent voice ask, 'Is Jack at your house? Er – this is Mrs Wilton speaking.'

'No, Jack is not here. What made you think he was?'

'I'll explain in a minute. Is Sarah there?'

'No, of course not. She went to stay overnight at your house.'

'I'm afraid that's not so. You see ...'

The two women went on chatting until they realized that both Jack and Sarah were missing. After the telephone conversation Mrs Thomas went to her husband who was in the sitting-room and said, 'Oh Alfred, she's run away, and Jack Wilton with her.'

'Who 'as?'

'Sarah – and it's because of you and the children.'

'What exactly d'you mean?'

'I mean that you have been shouting and bawling

at the poor girl and calling her names, and the children have been bullying and pestering her. I don't blame her for running away – but whatever shall we do when Mrs Parkinson comes back?'

Mr Thomas frowned. It would be in the papers. He would be blamed. He was responsible for Sarah. What if she was lost – wandering about in the streets – scared to come back! She could have been hurt, or run over, or even MURDERED! Masses of frightening pictures ran through his troubled mind. Oh dear! What a dreadful thing to happen!

'Alfred! This is what comes of your bad temper.'

Mr Thomas put his arm round his wife. 'I know, Fiona. If only we get Sarah back I will try to be better,' he moaned.

'Well, what are we going to do?'

'Phone the police.'

Meanwhile there was a disturbance at the circus camp.

'Where is Anna?' asked Jane Roland, eyeing the empty desk in the school caravan. 'Sam, go and look for her!'

The circus boy made his way to Anna's caravan with his dog at his heels. Sam hammered on the door which was opened by Anna's angry Ma.

'What is it? There's no need to make such a row.'

'My teacher wants Anna. Where is she?'

'She went down to the river last night to sleep on the old barge. I guess she's still there.'

Sam hurried across the field and down the stone steps to the river. What a shock he got! The barge had disappeared and there was no sign of Anna. For a moment the boy stood gaping. Then he came to his senses, and raced back to the field.

'The barge is gone!' he yelled to the circus folk, and the dog began to bark loudly. 'ANNA'S MISSING!' shrieked the boy.

There was a great hullabaloo, but the confused circus folk hastily pulled themselves together and arranged search parties to comb the river banks in a hunt for Anna and the barge.

Later that morning, up in the helicopter, the children saw through the windows a vast expanse of blue down below – they were flying over the sea! As time went by they sighted land half hidden by misty clouds and the helicopter began to descend. It landed at the edge of a wood, quite near to a fishing village.

Alf produced some large labels with something in French printed on them. He stuck them over the crate and then the two men carried the heavy object out of the helicopter, followed by the children and apes. They went a little way into the wood to where a landrover was parked behind some trees. The children could see that everything had been arranged well for the men. The three youngsters were bundled into the back of the vehicle together with the chimpanzees and the crate. Alf and Lianio leapt into the two front seats and Alf started the engine. He drove the landrover along a lane and into the fishing village. The street was cobbled and filled with busy crowds. Women in white aprons stood on the quay to greet the fishing boats which slid through the sea water heavily laden with wriggling

Suddenly Gepetto seemed to go mad

fish which slithered all over the decks. Merry fishermen called cheerily to one another, pleased with their catches.

Alf drove the landrover to the back of a white thatched bungalow. Here they stopped and unloaded the crate which was carried through the well-kept back garden where pink tamarisk grew. Alf kicked open the back door and they went into the kitchen, which had a black and white tiled floor and pale blue walls. The crate was put on the floor. The chimpanzees didn't like this strange house. It had a queer smell. Suddenly Gepetto seemed to go mad. His master didn't love him any more. He was in a horrid house he didn't like. He wanted to go back to the circus with its friendly folk, animals, familiar smells and good food. None of them had had anything to eat in the helicopter. Not one tin had been opened. It was too bad! Gepetto scurried into the hall and jumped on to a table, knocking over a china vase. He scampered into the sitting-room squealing loudly. There he tried to climb up a beautiful lace curtain. But, oh dear! There was a nasty tearing noise as the curtain ripped across the top and fell to the floor in a crumpled heap. Jessica joined in. She attempted to jump on to a bookcase and sent a clock, an ornament, and a chess set flying across the room. Gepetto began to pull the stuffing out of a cushion.

'Oh, my God!' cried Lianio. He and Alf, accompanied by the children, had already come racing in.

'These crazy chimps!' cried Alf. 'Whatever will Pierre say?'

Lianio made a grab at Jessica, who had just sent a tea-set crashing to the floor. There came the sound of running feet and an agitated voice cried, 'Alf! Ted! Is zat you? What ze 'eck is going on?'

At the sitting-room door appeared a little man with a tiny black moustache and short black hair. Just before he appeared Alf managed to hide some broken china under a rug and stuff the torn curtain under the sofa. But the man at the door could easily see by the crooked pictures on the wall, broken articles and vandalized furniture that his sitting-room had been completely wrecked.

chapter seven

Pierre and the treasure map

'Pierre, I can explain,' said Lianio, looking rather guilty.

'The chimps went mad,' said Alf, 'and they're not mine so don't glare at *me* like that. They're his.'

' 'Ave you brought ze watches?' Pierre asked. He spoke clearly and quite slowly. Because he was French and was used to speaking that language he tended to say 'z' instead of 'th'.

'Yes,' replied Lianio.

Pierre smiled. 'Zen soon I shall 'ave enough money to pay for zis damage,' he said. 'It does not matter. Come 'ere, little monkeys! I like you. You are sweet.'

Feeling doubtful, Gepetto went cautiously to the man and received a big hug. Pierre embraced and flattered the chimpanzees as if they were his own children. Then he noticed Jack, Sarah and Anna standing meekly in a corner.

'Who is zis boy and zese girls?' he asked.

'They found out what we were doing so we had to bring them in case they told the coppers,' explained Lianio.

'Who are ze coppers?'

'The police,' said Alf.

'Ah, yes, ze police. I will never remember zat English word "copper". I always zought it was a type of metal.'

Alf grinned at Lianio.

''Ave you got a place for 'em to sleep?' Alf asked.

'For who? A place for ze coppers to sleep?'

'No, for the kids.'

'Ah yes. Zey can sleep in ze loft. It is draughty but it will do.'

'Fine! Sorry about the damage.'

'Ah, Ted, it does not matter. Now zere is a roast chicken in ze oven. Ze table is set. Sit zere and ze monkeys and children shall sit round zat little table in ze corner. I will set it.'

Pierre left the room. A few minutes later a delicious smell floated in. The little man had brought in a dish containing a gorgeous chicken running in butter surrounded by roast potatoes and peas. The ravenous chimpanzees were provided with a supply of nuts and apples. After eating their meal in silence the children heard the men talk over cups of coffee.

Alf asked Pierre, ''Ave you got any spare beds?'

'No, only ones for you and Ted.'

'What about sleeping bags?' asked Lianio. 'The kids will need something to sleep in.'

'I 'ave no sleeping bags for zese children.'

'Any camp beds?'

'No, none at all.'

'Haven't you even got spare blankets?'

'Only one small one. Wait a minute. I 'ave some deck-chairs. Zey will do fine for beds.'

The children were not looking forward to a night

in the loft but there was still the afternoon to come. After lunch everyone went into the kitchen and Alf and Lianio opened the big crate. Out came trays crammed with wristwatches, gold ones, silver ones, watches with second hands, watches without, large ones, little ones, square ones and many others.

'Hurrah!' cried Pierre, examining a round gold watch. 'Zese are superb! *Wonderful!* BRAVO! Zey will look lovely in my shop window. I shall sell zem all for a good price. No one else in France shall 'ave such a superb jeweller's shop as I!'

'But remember these wristwatches are only yours when you give us the treasure map and lead us to Dubarry Castle,' said Lianio.

'Ze map is not absolutely correct,' said Pierre. 'I 'ave sent it to a friend to be checked over. Some of ze secret passages may not still be zere. But, ah, it will be a pleasure to exchange ze map for zese beautiful watches.'

'When will it be back?' asked Alf.

'Zis evening. Let us all go into ze garden.'

The children had been listening carefully. It was clear that Alf and Lianio had smuggled stolen watches over to France to exchange for a treasure map. Pierre, the owner of the map, was going to open a new jeweller's shop and was pleased to exchange his map for some watches he could sell.

Pierre had a delightful garden. Flowers bloomed everywhere and young trees sprouted from soil that was dry because of the hot sun. Pierre set out some deck-chairs and draped a sunhat over his head. Everyone sat down. Soon quiet snoring was heard

'I will tell you ze 'istory of my family and myself'

as Alf, and then Lianio, fell asleep in the hot sun. The chimpanzees curled up under a shady bush and were soon dreaming of stuffy helicopters, nasty men, barges, and appetizing nuts and apples.

Only Pierre and the children were left awake. The Frenchman beckoned Sarah saying, 'You are very pretty. Come and sit on my knee.'

Sarah went doubtfully and sat on Pierre's lap with the Frenchman's arm round her.

'I will tell you ze 'istory of my family and myself,' said the man. 'One of my ancestors 'ad a brozer-in-law who owned a fine castle called Dubarry Castle. It lies a few kilometres from 'ere and is only a ruin but 'as secret entrances everywhere. My great-great-great-grandfazer made a map of zis fine place including all ze passages. But in most of zem ze roofs 'ave collapsed causing zem to be blocked up. Ze map 'as been passed down ze family to me and shows dungeons where treasure is supposed to be 'idden. Ze castle is built on a cliff and ze dungeons are in ze cliff. I 'ave not sought for zis treasure because if I ever found it it would 'ave to go straight to a museum. Besides' – he lowered his voice – 'I do not really believe zat zere is any treasure at all. If zere was, why didn't my great-great-great grandfazer find it when 'e made ze map? My friend, Yves, 'ad a great-uncle who also looked for ze treasure, but in vain. 'Owever' – he glanced at the two men to make sure they were asleep – 'your friends, Alf and Ted, are convinced zat zere is treasure! Per'aps zey will find it!' But Pierre spoke the last sentence with a definite lack of enthusiasm and a sardonic smile flickered over his face.

'When was Dubarry Castle in use?' asked Sarah, breaking the short silence after Pierre's speech.

'In ze days when knights were bold. Ze castle belonged to ze famous Duke Henri Dubarry. I will tell you ze legend of ze castle and ze treasure when ze map arrives tonight.'

After thinking for a moment Jack said, 'If your ancestor's brother-in-law owned Dubarry Castle, then your name can't be Dubarry.'

'No, it is Dupont. You children will call me Mr Dupont. Ah! Ze men are awakening.'

Lianio stirred, opened his eyes, blinked and asked, 'How long have I been asleep?'

'About ten minutes,' replied Mr Dupont.

The rest of the afternoon the party slept in the sun, wandered round the garden and chatted. The children had taken a liking to Mr Dupont. He was friendly, kindly, funny and gay. It was a pity that he was in league with Alf and Lianio who were burglars, smugglers and kidnappers.

That evening it got rather chilly so everyone went inside and had salad for supper. Around nine o'clock Alf was in the hall when he saw an envelope lying on the carpet by the front door. He snatched it up, and tearing it open cried, 'Pierre! It's come!'

Mr Dupont came running over with Lianio, followed by the children. Pierre grabbed the envelope from Alf and pulled out a letter and a folded piece of paper, throwing the envelope to the floor. Evidently the letter had been delivered by hand as, apart from Mr Dupont's name written on the front, there was no address or stamp.

Everyone went into the dining-room and sat round the table. There was a small note written in French.

'I suppose I shall 'ave to translate zis for you,' Mr Dupont remarked to Alf and Lianio.

This is what the note said:

Dear Pierre,
Your old map was so worn out that I had to make a new copy. I have indicated any blocked-up passages with a red line. I have done my best to make the map as clear and correct as possible, but even now there may be some mistakes as my own map is several years old, though not as ancient as yours. Good luck when you hunt for the treasure.
Yours sincerely,
Yves Gerard

'You see,' explained Mr Dupont, 'Yves 'as a map as well. 'Is great-uncle made one and as it is not so old as mine it is more likely to be correct. Now let us see zis map. Come along, children.'

'They don't need to see,' said Alf.

'Yes, zey do,' argued Mr Dupont, spreading the map out on the table.

'Well, I'm glad you're taking a liking to them,' said Lianio, 'because when we leave France we want you to keep them for a while. Then when we are far away you can let 'em loose in the streets.'

Mr Dupont looked doubtful and said, 'Let us change ze subject. Look at ze map.'

Six pairs of eyes stared at the sheet of paper

Six pairs of eyes stared at the sheet of paper. It showed a ruined castle on a cliff with red marks everywhere. Mr Dupont pointed to one part of the cliff saying, 'Zis is where ze dungeons are. Ze proper entrance to zese dungeons used to lead down from inside ze castle, but one of ze castle towers collapsed on top of it so zat it cannot be used now. Zere are two ozer entrances, 'owever, which no one but us and Yves knows about. Firstly zere is an iron door in ze side of ze cliff. Zis door is 'idden by nettles and bracken.' He placed his finger on the map. 'Zat is where ze iron door stands. Ze second entrance' – pointing to another spot on the map – 'is 'ere. It is a tunnel leading from ze outside of ze cliff to ze dungeons. You see, zere used to be an underground stream running zere a long, long time ago and ze water 'as worn away ze rock leaving a narrow tunnel. As you see Yves 'as put red marks zrough zese black lines representing secret passages. Zis means zat now all ze passages are blocked up.'

'But look! There is a passage with no red mark through it,' said Lianio, tracing his finger along a black line which trailed right off the edge of the paper.

'So zere is. Zat one must be unblocked, but it goes right off ze edge of ze paper and ze map does not show where it ends. It is not much use to us zen. Ze best entrance for us to use is ze iron door.'

' 'Ow did all these passages get there in the first place?' queried Alf.

'Well, I will tell you ze legend. Ze Dubarrys lived in ze castle and owned an 'oard of valuable treasure.

Many ozers wished to steal zis famous treasure and zat made ze Dubarrys afraid. So zey carried zeir treasure down to ze dungeons and 'id it zere carefully. Soon an army of Duponts came forward 'oping to capture ze castle and ze treasure. Ze Dubarrys were outnumbered and so ze Duponts took ze castle and put ze Dubarry prisoners into ze dungeons. Ze prisoners dug tunnels out of ze dungeons and escaped by zese. Zat is 'ow all ze secret passages got zere.'

'But why didn't the prisoners take their treasure with them?' asked Anna.

Mr Dupont laughed loudly. 'My dear, it would be far too 'eavy! Per'aps zey took a few bags of gold or jewels zough. Ze Duponts never found ze treasure. Zoze of zem who were left lived in ze castle until zey were driven out by anozer family. After zat, ze castle fell into disuse, because it 'ad been so badly damaged during all ze fighting. So ze treasure is still zere, under ze castle. Now you, Ted and Alf, are going to find it – and it will look lovely in a museum. Glittering cups, armour, silver plates . . .'

Lianio scowled and muttered, 'You know very well we didn't steal those watches so that we could send the treasure to a bloomin' museum.'

Pierre laughed in amusement. 'Ah, Ted, you know I am only pulling ze leg! Eh, children?'

'It's time those kids went to bed,' growled Alf.

At half past nine the children were alone, lying in deck-chairs in the loft. Mr Dupont had just left after saying 'goodnight'. Sarah was covered by a blanket, the others had rugs over them, and all three had cushions for pillows. A small skylight let in some evening sunshine. Although the time was half past nine, the summer day was not yet over.

The loft was respectably clean, without cobwebs or earwigs. There were various sized boxes and cases piled up against the rafters.

'Oh dear!' moaned Sarah. 'What will happen to us?'

'Don't worry,' said Anna. 'Worrying never does anyone any good.'

'Nor does fear,' groaned poor Sarah. 'It's all my fault. If I hadn't been scared to face Mr Thomas we'd never have gone to sleep on that wretched barge.'

'It wasn't your fault,' said Anna. 'It was my idea to sleep there.'

'I shouldn't have gone, and I shouldn't have let you go either,' said Jack.

'Well, Mr Dupont is quite nice,' said Anna, hoping for the best. 'He might help us to escape when Lianio and Alf leave France.'

'I used to like Lianio,' said Sarah. 'He seemed kind and friendly. Now he's a smuggler.'

'And a burglar.'

'And a kidnapper. As for Alf – he's the worst of the lot, isn't he, girls?'

'Yes, he wanted to leave us locked up in that helicopter place.'

Sarah yawned. 'Let's get some sleep. Goodness knows what we will be doing tomorrow.'

'Yes,' said Jack. 'Goodnight, Sarah. Goodnight, Anna.'

' 'Night, Jack.'

After their long day of excitement and adventure the children soon dropped off to sleep.

chapter eight

The treasure-hunt

They woke in the morning to hear the sweet singing of birds perched on the eaves of the roof. The sun shone strongly through the skylight brightening up the loft.

'I hope we're getting some breakfast,' said Jack, looking at his watch. 'It's nine o'clock.'

'Maybe Mr Dupont doesn't get up till late,' suggested Sarah.

'No, I can hear someone moving about below,' said Anna.

'Well, I'm going down,' said Sarah, throwing aside her blanket and sitting up.

'Better not!' said Jack. 'Alf or Lianio might be cross.'

'I'm not scared,' said Sarah boldly, stepping out of the deck-chair. 'I've made up my mind to be brave. Because I was frightened of Mr Thomas we ended up here. I shan't be frightened any more.'

She climbed out of the loft and went towards the kitchen. Suddenly she bumped into Alf.

'Who told you to get up?' he bawled. 'Get back to bed!'

Poor Sarah couldn't help being nervous. 'I – I'm n-not scared of y-*you*,' she stammered.

Putting his hands on his hips Alf said coldly, 'You aren't, aren't you? Well, let me tell you this, young madam, I don't think much of cheeky kids like you, so – GET BACK TO BED!'

Sarah scuttled off like a frightened rabbit. Alf had put a stop to her 'bravery'. Jack and Anna were just descending from the loft.

'You're not allowed out,' said Sarah.

'We had better just wait, then.'

At a quarter to ten the children were given a breakfast consisting of crusty French bread with jam, and mugs of cocoa.

'Today we shall all go to ze castle and seek for ze treasure,' Mr Dupont told them, as he brought the meal in on a tray. If the children had been told this at home by one of their parents the statement would have delighted them. But they did not want to go with strange men they didn't like.

But what was going on at home? Let us go back to the previous day. Since Sarah's disappearance a great change had come over Mr Thomas. He groaned as he thought back over all the wicked things he had said and done. It was a wonder that his wife had not divorced him. He decided to turn over a new leaf, and even proposed taking his wife and children to church the following Sunday. In bed at night he thought over all the ways in which he could improve.

Molly, Billy and Mark were surprised to find that their father scolded them if they were rude to Mrs Thomas, unkind, selfish or greedy. Previously he would have approved of their wicked ways, but now he told them, 'It is wrong to be bad and selfish. Has anyone ever been really nasty to *you*?'

'No.'

'Well, why be nasty to other people? No one will like you, and God wants you to be kind and loving to others.'

Normally when the children were told something, the words went in one ear and slipped out of the other. But this speech of their father's stuck in their heads. Mrs Thomas was glad to see the gradual change coming over her children. But she and her husband were still very worried about Sarah.

The police had been told and it was in the newspapers. There were three photographs of the children and a short passage under each giving names, addresses, and details of where the children had last been seen. Anna's Ma wasn't pleased at having her daughter's picture in the papers. Mr Jimminy had returned to the circus without Lianio.

'You see, halfway there Lianio wanted to split up so he could go a short cut and buy food for the chimps on the way,' explained Mr Jimminy. 'He said the short cut was muddy and marshy so I just carried on the way I was going, expecting to meet him at the fair. But he wasn't there. I just couldn't find him. That's all I can tell you folks.'

The circus folk were unhappy and worried.

'We can't have this!' bellowed the Ringmaster. 'Lianio was one of our star attractions. Why, for heaven's sake, hasn't he come back?'

This was a question which nobody but Sarah,

Anna, Jack, Alf, Mr Dupont and Lianio himself could answer.

Meanwhile, in France, the children had finished breakfast and were being taken to the same land-rover that had been hidden in the forest for Alf and Lianio after the helicopter ride. The vehicle was evidently Pierre's. The sun had been blazing through the windows on to the front seats making them boiling hot, so that Alf and Mr Dupont, the driver, jumped when they sat down. The children and Lianio clambered into the back. The doors were slammed shut and the windows opened wide to let in some fresh air. The chimpanzees were left behind, tied up in the garden, so that they could not get up to mischief. The landrover was even hotter and stuffier than the helicopter. Mr Dupont drove along uneven roads which wound up a rocky hill. The landrover rocked and bumped up and down as it went over the humpy tracks. Soon they had gone down the other side of the rocky hill and were crossing hard, dry fields. Jerking to and fro, and hitting stones, the landrover rolled on, leaving wide tyre tracks behind it. Alf had a plastic box containing sandwiches on his lap. Evidently they were staying until after lunch. The treasure map was tucked into Mr Dupont's pocket and the French-man drove his vehicle through an open gate out of the fields. Now they were going along a wide gravel path. Grit and gravel flew up hitting the sides of the landrover and falling back on to the path. Mr Dupont excitedly pointed a finger towards a hump in the distance. 'Ze cliff! Ze cliff!' he cried. 'Wiz ze castle on ze top!'

Alf leant forward and peered through the windscreen. After ten minutes of driving the castle could be seen clearly. It was built on a steep, jagged cliff and, because of rocks which had tumbled down its side blocking the roadway, Mr Dupont had to stop the landrover. 'We will climb now,' he said, getting the map out of his pocket.

Everyone got out and looked at the massive cliff. On top they perceived a ruined castle. It was built of reddish-brown stone and only had slits for windows. This had prevented the enemy's arrows from getting into the castle easily and protected the archers while firing their own arrows from inside. One of the walls had tumbled to the ground and lay there slowly crumbling away. Three tall stiff towers still remained but one of these was rotting badly. There was not much left of the great wooden doors which had once been the entrance to Dubarry castle. The dungeons were beneath the building, in the cliff. Their former entrance had been blocked up when the fourth tower had collapsed on top of it. Now they had to find other ways in. Would the treasure still be there? If so, would they be able to find it?

They all began to walk to the cliff, scrambling over loose rocks. Mr Dupont examined the map and they all followed him up the cliff. The hard, hot rocks hurt the children's feet and it was difficult to keep up with the men, who strode ahead.

'According to zis,' remarked Mr Dupont, inspect-

The men came running up in delight

ing the map, 'ze iron door is somewhere in zis area. Start searching, everyone. You, children, too.'

They began scrambling about the cliff, kicking loose bits of stone down the side. Rock walls were knocked on to discover if they were hollow or not. Stones were pushed aside, but nothing like a door was underneath, and caves were searched. After half an hour it became tiring and the children sat on rocks to rest. Their hands were scratched and they all wanted a cold drink. But their attention was drawn from self-pity to Alf who was shouting. He was in a large recess in the cliff where bracken and ferns covered the rock surface. The excited man was tearing the plants away and revealing a patch of rusty iron. Lianio and Mr Dupont came running up in delight and helped to tear away the bracken and ferns. Soon a heap of dead plants lay on the rock floor. In the recess was an iron door with rusty hinges and a rusty handle. Alf turned the handle and pushed the door with no success. He kicked the door and succeeded in hurting his foot. Mr Dupont grinned. 'Ah! Poor, poor Alf,' he laughed.

'Pity *you* can't open it,' said Alf bitterly. Mr Dupont grabbed the handle and gave the door a great shove. Nothing happened. His grin faded away. 'It is locked,' he said. 'Zere are bolts on ze inside. Who can 'ave moved zem across ze door?'

Lianio sighed wearily and said, 'It's probably been locked since the map was made.'

'Well, for heaven's sake let's go in through the secret passage,' said Alf.

'But no one knows where it ends,' remarked Mr Dupont. 'It goes right off ze map.'

'There's that tunnel thing,' said Lianio carelessly.

'Yes, we will use zat,' said Mr Dupont. 'Follow me!'

They all climbed over the lumpy rocks to the right of the cliff. Then another hunt began. After seeking for twenty minutes the children felt that they had been in absolutely every nook and cranny. Sweat covered their faces. It was all horrid. The sun was too hot. The cliff was too hard. Their feet felt painful, and it looked as if the tunnel, let alone the treasure, would never be found.

'Hey, you kids!' called Alf from not far off. 'Stop resting! Keep looking and don't dawdle!'

The children sighed. They wished they didn't have to be ordered about. They wished they were at home. The girls hardly searched at all because they were completely worn out. But Jack climbed on to a rock ledge and what should he spy but a hole half hidden by bracken! The boy peeped in and saw a tunnel leading through the darkness. He knew it must be what the men were looking for but he wasn't going to tell them. They would find the treasure and sell it. It would look much nicer on velvet cushions in glass cases in a museum. Jack decided to hide the hole with more bracken, and looked round for some. He saw Alf standing below, shading his eyes from the sun as he peered up. 'Ted! Pierre!' called the man. 'This kid's found it!'

Jack was annoyed. His plan was spoiled and the treasure would fall into the evil hands of Alf and Lianio. By now the men had scrambled on to the ledge and, pushing Jack aside, tore away the bracken. A dark tunnel stretched out before them. Alf stuck his head in, holding a powerful torch in his hand, but his hefty shoulders would not go through the hole. Even small Mr Dupont could not squeeze in. The men were in despair. But suddenly Lianio suggested, 'Couldn't these kids go in? When they reach the dungeons they can unbolt the iron door for us.'

'They might escape,' said Alf.

'No, someone will guard this entrance and the other two of us can wait outside the iron door,' explained Lianio. 'Unless the kids let us in they'll starve in the dungeons. They can't escape. If they tried they'd get lost. They wouldn't know what to do – they're too young.'

'That ain't a bad idea,' said Alf.

So Pierre took out the map and explained to the children how they would get to the iron door. 'Zere is a long passage,' he said. 'At one end is a staircase leading up to ze place where a tower collapsed on ze old entrance. At ze ozer end of ze passage is ze iron door. On eizer side of ze passage zere are dungeons wiz zick walls separating zem. Ze doors to ze dungeons are all in ze passage, but as zey are all broken down you can move about as you please. You will go along ze tunnel and into ze first dungeon. Zen all you 'ave to do is to come out of ze dungeon zrough ze broken-down door and into ze

passage. Walk to ze end of ze passage and zen unbolt
ze iron door. Now, no fooling about when you are
inside or you may get lost!'

Soon the children were crawling awkwardly on
painful hands and knees. Jack crept along in front
of the girls with Alf's torch in his hand. The bright
torchlight showed them the way. A foul smell hung
in the air and it was surprisingly cold. At last the
tunnel opened out into the first dungeon as Pierre
had said and the children were able to stretch their
aching limbs. Jack flashed the torch over the musty
walls and mud floor of the dungeon.

'There's that broken-down door leading into the
passage,' said Sarah. 'Coming?'

'No,' replied Anna. 'Let the men wait. They've
been cruel to us. Now let's get our own back. We'll
be nasty to them and keep them waiting. I want to
look for the treasure myself. Pierre said all the
dungeon doors are broken down, so we can easily
hunt for the treasure and go where we want.'

'Yes, I'd like to look for the treasure too,' said
Sarah, 'but – won't the men be angry if we take a
long time?'

'We won't let them in,' said Anna decidedly.

'Don't be silly!' snapped Jack. 'You know very
well that wouldn't help anyone. We've got nothing
to eat, and we should never find our way out except
by the iron door and the tunnel. Don't try to get us
into a worse mess than we are in already!'

'Couldn't we open the iron door, push past the
men and—' began Anna.

'No, we couldn't! Do stop making silly suggestions! Can't you see that we are in enough danger as it is?'

Anna sighed. 'Well, there's nothing wrong in looking for the treasure, is there?'

'Not really. It would be quite fun. If we found it we might be able to keep the men away from it and draw their attention somewhere else when they start hunting.'

'Yes! Yes! Sarah, we can tell the men that we had difficulty getting through the tunnel. Anyway, they won't mind us taking a long time. They'll be more interested in finding the treasure.'

'True,' said Sarah. 'Come on then!'

They trooped through the dungeon door and found the passage that Pierre had spoken of. Sure enough, there was the iron door at the end. But the children turned their backs on it and entered the second dungeon. It wasn't very exciting, though. All the dungeons seemed to have the same old mud floor and filthy walls. They wandered into the fourth dungeon and walked out. Suddenly Jack put his foot down and the floor beneath it seemed to wobble. Jack was puzzled. He flashed Alf's torch on the ground and took another step forward. Again the floor appeared to move a little. Jack called the girls over and they scrabbled about on the ground. They found that the mud floor had crumbled away, revealing some wooden planks. These had wobbled when Jack had stepped on them. The children wondered why. They brushed the lumps of mud to one side with their hands and examined the wooden boards carefully. What were planks doing under the

They gasped and peered more closely

dungeon floor? Then, as Jack flashed the torch over the boards, Anna's sharp eyes spotted something gleaming through the cracks and gaps in the wood. They gasped and peered more closely. Could it be ...? It MUST be ...! It HAD to be ... the treasure! It was not too difficult to move all the planks to one side. The children goggled as they saw that a great square pit had been dug in the mud floor and then covered up with planks and mud. The pit was filled up with that beautiful, long-lost treasure. So this was where the Dubarrys had cleverly hidden their hoard! No wonder it had never been found – and how lucky they were to have discovered it accidentally! The mud must have begun to crumble away with age and the wood have rotted. Jack jumped down into the pit first, and the girls followed. The square pit was so huge that they were able to walk around inside it and examine the treasure.

Bronze, decorated chests were overflowing with hoards of glittering gold coins and creamy pearls. Gleaming silver cups studded with bright gems rested among large heaps of golden dishes with designs engraved on them. Tall, elegant vases were crammed with sapphire rings, shining bracelets, ruby brooches, pearl necklaces and other precious jewels – much to the delight of the girls. Jack admired the gleaming swords and daggers with shining hilts and sheaths elaborately adorned with precious stones. Shields with all kinds of fascinating designs lay in piles and there were some sacks of coins stacked in one corner of the pit. The suits of armour which lay around the chests were rather rusted over after all the years but looked just like real knights at rest. The children had never seen anything so wonderful before. They gazed at everything and ran pearls and jewels through their fingers. The girls tried on some necklaces and rings while Jack slipped swords in and out of their sheaths. But suddenly they caught their breaths in fright as a bright beam of torchlight was flashed upon them from above and an agitated voice cried, 'James! It is children! What are *zey* doing 'ere?'

chapter nine

Mrs Pompidou

The children looked up quickly and perceived three people standing at the edge of the pit. As they soon realized from their accents, there was a French man and woman and an American man.

'Gee, baby!' remarked the American. 'These youngsters have sure helped us find the treasure, yeah?'

'Yes,' agreed the Frenchwoman. 'But what are you going to do wiz zem, Yves?'

Leaning over the edge of the pit, the Frenchman called Yves snapped something in French at the children.

'What is he saying, Jack?' asked Anna quietly.

'What? You are English?' exclaimed Yves in surprise. 'Get out of zat pit!'

It was only then that the children realized that they were stuck. The pit was quite deep and there was no ladder or anything to help them up. However, Yves and the American stretched down their arms, caught Anna and Sarah by the hands and pulled them up. But Jack managed to scramble up by himself as he was the tallest.

'Why are you 'ere?' snapped Yves, as the three sullen children stood in a row before him. Jack remembered that Yves was the man who had corrected Pierre's map.

'We came with Pierre Dupont and two others,' answered Jack. Then something occurred to him. 'Hey! How did you get in?'

'Zat is none of your business. You say Pierre is 'ere? Where is 'e?'

'He's waiting for us to unbolt the iron door,' replied Jack.

'Ha! Ha!' laughed Yves. 'I tricked 'im nicely! Ha! Ha!'

Curiosity gave Jack the courage to ask, 'What do you mean? You corrected his map. Did you make it all wrong?'

'You know a lot,' said Yves. 'Too much for my liking. No, I did not make Pierre's map *all* wrong. Zis is what I did. Zere is an unblocked passage which we used. I put a red line zrough it on Pierre's map so 'e zinks it is blocked. But it isn't really. It leads into ze zird dungeon. Zat is 'ow we got in. But' – his face broke into a frown – 'I 'ave told you too much. Now I cannot let you go. If I do you will let Pierre and 'is friends in. I do not want zis. I want ze treasure for myself. It shall go to no rotten museum. I shall melt down ze precious metals and sell zem. I will be rich, *rich*, RICH! Swimming in coins!'

'Yeah!' agreed the American. 'But you're sure givin' me plen'y, remember, buddy! It's me who's meltin' it down fer you!'

None of the children liked the American. The gun stuck in his belt made Sarah shiver. Jack knew that guns could be bought in America without a licence, so the boy reckoned that this American had smuggled his gun over to France.

'Now, James,' said the Frenchman to the American, 'what can we do wiz zese children while we load ze treasure on to our lorry round ze back of ze cliff?'

'Shut them up in one of the dungeons, buddy. Remember the one where bits of the wall have collapsed in places, and there are rocks lyin' all around? Well, we can block up the doorway with rocks – OK?'

'Very well, zen. Get on wiz it. Take zese children away while I get into ze pit and pass some of ze stuff up to Cécile. 'Urry up so zat you can come and 'elp me move some of ze 'eavy chests.'

The hefty American pushed the children along in front of him out of the treasure dungeon and into another. The poor children watched in despair as the doorway was gradually blocked up with big stones, far too heavy for them to move. Alf's torch had been taken from them so it was very dark although there was a faint light, which got in through gaps between the rocks at the doorway, from a lantern which Yves had placed in the main passage to help them see while they were moving the treasure. The place was smelly, musty and damp. Puddles covered the floor because when it was wet rain seeped through cracks in the cliff and gathered in the dungeon. The children felt utterly miserable. Not even the chimpanzees were there to cheer them up. The floor was slimy and the walls made you shiver if you touched them for they were icy cold.

The children watched in despair as the doorway was gradually blocked up

They hadn't the tiniest crumb of food to eat and they were feeling hungry. Why, oh why, had this fate befallen them? Their captors did not look at all nice. Yves had a thin, spiteful-looking face with fierce eyes, a black moustache and a mop of black, shiny hair. The American was plump, with glittering white teeth, and that awful gun in his belt. His brown hair was much lighter than Cécile's, who had a thin nose and a receding chin. She wore a tight-fitting green dress and black stockings.

All three children stood leaning on the musty, damp dungeon walls, thinking hard. As their eyes got used to the darkness, Jack saw an ancient battle-axe lying on the mud floor. It had a metal blade and a wooden handle. Jack bent over, picked up the axe and tapped it on the wall carelessly, saying, 'We could dig an escape tunnel with this.' To his surprise, where he had hit the wall a whole lot of rubble and stone tumbled to the floor leaving a gaping hole. The three astonished children squatted before the hole and Anna remarked, 'If all the wall is as rotten as this we can dig our way out.'

'Do you know what I think?' cried Sarah excitedly.

'What?'

'I think that this is the entrance to one of those blocked-up passages that someone has hidden with bits of rock.'

'Good thinking, old girl,' said Jack.

'But I don't see what good a blocked-up passage will do us,' said Anna miserably.

'Well,' considered Jack, 'we might be able to unblock it with this axe.'

But they were all doubtful.

'Look!' said Anna, snatching the battleaxe. 'This thing is no use. It's years old.' She hacked at the wall with the axe and the handle broke off.

'Clever girl,' said Jack sarcastically. 'We might have been able to use that.'

'Of course we couldn't,' said Anna indignantly. 'It's an ancient thing.'

'Well, I still wish you hadn't broken—'

'Oh, stop arguing, you two!' interrupted Sarah. 'I agree with Anna – the thing's of no use.'

'Let's go down the passage,' said Anna. 'At least it's something to do, and if it's not badly blocked up we might be able to clear it with our bare hands.'

She was already crawling in at the entrance. It would have helped if a light could have been provided, but there was none.

'The roof might fall in,' said Jack urgently. 'Come out, Anna!'

'It's only fallen in once,' said a muffled voice from the passage, 'so why should it fall in *now* on top of me?'

'How do you know it has only fallen in once ...?' began Jack, but then he saw Sarah going into the passage and thought he'd better follow.

The tunnel was pitch dark and its walls and roof were rock. The children had to feel with their hands to make sure they were going straight. The tunnel gave very faint echoes of their footsteps as they made their way along the rock floor.

'It's spooky!' whispered Sarah.

'I don't think so,' said Jack aloud. 'Why are you whispering, Sarah?'

'I don't know. I feel this is a place where you ought to whisper.'

'Idiot!' laughed Anna. 'Strange to think that prisoners have escaped in the very tunnel we're walking in.'

'I wonder if we're near the blockage,' said Sarah.

'Yes, I hope we don't suddenly bump into it,' said Jack. 'Wish we'd got a light.'

'Oops!' cried Anna, as she stumbled over something and fell to the ground.

'Are you OK?' asked Jack.

'Yes.' Anna was feeling the thing she had toppled over. 'It's an old torch. A stick of wood that was lit at the top. They used 'em for light – 'cept this one isn't lit.'

'Drat! I don't have any matches,' moaned Jack.

'Same here.'

'Same here.'

'Well, I'll chuck this wood away, then.'

Soon they were all walking again. Sometimes they could stand straight; once or twice they had to bend their heads, and often had to crawl. Gradually, the tunnel's walls, roof and floor became earth. They had walked through the rock cliff and were now beneath soil. Suddenly Jack exclaimed, 'Do you think this could be the passage that isn't blocked?'

'No, it can't be,' said Anna. 'They wouldn't put us in the dungeon that has the secret passage that they got in by.'

'No,' argued Sarah excitedly. 'This could be the *other* unblocked passage. There are two, Anna. One ends in the third dungeon – Yves used that. The other just goes off the edge of the map – remember? No one knows where it ends. Yves must have forgotten it when he shut us up. Oh, we've had so much bad luck, I do hope we have some good luck, don't you?'

'Yes, yes, I ...' Just then Anna bumped into a dead-end. 'Oh no! It's a blockage,' she groaned.

'It's not,' said Sarah, feeling the earth. 'It's the end of the passage, that's all. We'll feel around for an exit.'

'Oh great! We're nearly free!' cried Jack. He felt about on the roof, and suddenly his hands went through it. He could feel grass. 'Here's the exit!' he cried. 'It's a hole, all covered up with plants and stuff.'

Thick nettles and tangled plants had grown over the exit so that it was difficult to stretch them apart and make room to get out. Jack's hands were very scratched when he finally pushed away the last few bits of undergrowth and greenery, revealing a patch of daylight which streamed into the passage. The girls squealed in delight. How beautiful that daylight seemed to them!

'How do we get up?' asked Anna.

Jack looked round. 'Aha!' he said, spotting some footholds going up the earth wall. The boy climbed up and stepped out of the hole, followed by the girls. They were expecting it to be sunny but it had turned chilly and was spitting with rain. They had come out a little way from someone's garden, in a corner of a field where the grass nearly reached their knees. The children decided to go over to the house to look for help. As they climbed over the garden hedge someone gave a startled cry and the children saw a plump Frenchwoman taking down her washing because of the rain. She wore a yellow blouse, and a white apron over a skirt which stuck out slightly because of the many petticoats underneath. Her brown hair, with a few grey wisps, was tied in a bun on top of her head. The woman had rosy cheeks and big blue eyes. She rattled off something in French.

'Er – we're English,' said Jack, hoping the woman knew his language. She did.

' 'Ow did you get 'ere?' she snapped. ' 'Ow dare you come barging into my garden?'

'Sorry, madame,' Jack apologized. 'We've come along a passage from Dubarry castle. I can see the building from here. We've had a most fascinating adventure and it's a matter for the police.'

The Frenchwoman looked doubtfully at Jack and asked to see the passage. She obviously thought they were lying. They led the angry woman to the corner of the field assuring her that they were telling the truth. The woman looked into the hole and said, 'Forgive me for my 'arsh words. My name is Madame Pompidou. You will prefer to call me Mrs Pompidou. Please come into my 'ouse and tell me your story.'

Sarah didn't like going with strangers, but, as Jack and Anna were going towards the house, she followed. Mrs Pompidou had quickly taken down her remaining washing and put it in the kitchen in its basket.

'Now tell me zis strange tale,' she said when they were all sitting comfortably in armchairs. Jack began, and with the girls helping him told the story briefly.

'You mean to say zat zose criminals are still in ze dungeons?' asked the flustered Mrs Pompidou when the tale had been completed.

'Yes,' said Anna.

'Zen I must phone ze police,' cried the Frenchwoman, and ran into the hall where she grabbed the telephone receiver. She dialled a number and spoke hasty words in French into the telephone. Then she returned to the lounge and sank into a chair saying, 'Zey are coming. You children are very brave to 'ave zese zings 'appening to you.'

Suddenly there came a knocking on the door. Mrs Pompidou jumped to her feet crying, 'Ze police!'

She ran to the door and opened it. But it wasn't the police. A tall youth with black hair, wearing a hat and a coat covered in rainwater, stepped in and put his briefcase on the floor. There was a short conversation in French while Mrs Pompidou helped the young man take off his soaked coat and hat. Then the couple came into the lounge and Mrs Pompidou announced, 'Children, zis is my son, Louis.'

The youth sat down and he and his mother spoke to each other for a moment in French. The children did not like this. It made them suspicious to see Mrs Pompidou talking of something they could not understand. What if Mrs Pompidou was in league with the criminals? Had she *really* phoned the police, or had she phoned the man whom she claimed to be her son? Was the youth really her son, Louis, or was he another criminal? Jack wasn't keen to explain things when Louis asked him to tell of their adventure.

'Well – er – it began with – er – er – a barge. You see, well ...' He stopped when there came a loud knock on the door.

'Ze police at last,' said Mrs Pompidou, and this time it was. The French police wore navy blue uniforms with silver buttons and carried guns. Their hats were shaped like large blue pillboxes with peaks.

'Well, I 'ear you 'ave an interesting story to tell,' said the policeman who seemed to the children to be in charge.

'Yes,' said Jack. 'It began when ...' It didn't take the children long to tell their tale. When it was finished the police asked to see the secret passage. They all went down and made their way through, but Mrs Pompidou stayed behind. The police went stealthily down the tunnel with their guns pointed in front of them, followed by the children and Louis. Who should they meet halfway down the tunnel but Yves, Cécile and the American! They had discovered that the children were gone and, after finding the passage, had come down to look for them. Much to their astonishment they fell into

The police asked to see the secret passage

the hands of the police on their way through. The policeman in charge said something in French and then the sullen trio was led out along the passage, all handcuffed, by a few of the policemen. They had been searching for these people for a long time as they were wanted criminals who had committed many robberies together in France.

The remaining policemen had a plan. Having heard that the other criminals, Alf, Lianio and Pierre, were waiting for the iron door to be opened, one policeman slid back the bolts while others stood blocking the passage, as the children looked on. The impatient villains rushed in and gasped in surprise at the sight of the police. Before they knew it they were surrounded by a group of Frenchmen in dark uniforms armed with guns. Alf tried to push past one man but was given a rough shove and backed into Lianio and Pierre.

While the crooks were being driven away to cells the children had been taken back to Mrs Pompidou's house and were tucking into a good meal. Although it was long past lunch time Mrs Pompidou had been sharp enough to realize that they had had no midday meal and so she had prepared a tasty snack. For the three adventurers it was a relief to feel safe, but how would they get home?

chapter ten

Back home

That afternoon, poor Mrs Pompidou's house was crowded with men who wanted photographs and information about the children for newspapers and television.

Louis turned out to be a kindly youth. His best friend, Jacques Durand, was the captain of a ferry. It was arranged for the children to travel over to Britain on this ferry which would arrive at Dover. After this news of their homeward voyage, the children felt as if a great weight had slipped off their shoulders, so they were very relieved and happy during the rest of the day.

When most of the interviewers and photographers had gradually disappeared, the police arrived with a large map of the area. They wished to retrieve the crate of stolen watches from Pierre's home and asked the children to give them further details about the house and to explain whereabouts it stood. Using the map and their memories, Jack, Sarah and Anna managed to do so.

But just as the police were getting ready to leave, Anna cried, 'Wait! There are two chimpanzees tied up in Pierre's garden. You must bring them back ...', and she told them all about Gepetto and

Jessica. The police promised to fetch the apes and said that they would arrange somehow for the animals to be returned to the circus. The children had also been asked their full names and addresses so that their parents could be informed of their safety.

The police left, but it was not long before someone else arrived. This time it was Mrs Pompidou's husband who had just come home from work. He was as friendly as his wife and son, and fascinated to hear of the children's escapades.

At six o'clock some pictures of Jack, Sarah and Anna were shown on the television news. The French newsreader was talking all about the treasure, the children, the castle and the criminals. Although the three youngsters could not understand the newsreader's language, they saw pictures of the Dubarry treasure being loaded into a lorry to be taken to a museum.

All too soon, bedtime came. The girls slept in a big spare double-bed while Jack kept nice and warm in a sleeping-bag. Mrs Pompidou provided night-clothes, and mugs of hot chocolate. It was comforting to lay their weary heads on soft pillows and let their eyes close. They dropped off to sleep instantly, worn out after their exciting day of adventure.

At breakfast the next morning, the Pompidous explained things to them. Louis informed them that the ferry was leaving the harbour at eleven o'clock. Mr Pompidou told them what had happened to Jessica and Gepetto. 'Zey 'ad gnawed zrough ze ropes which tied zem up in ze garden,' he said. 'Zis is what ze police told me while you were asleep. When zey were free, zey ran all over ze garden looking for food. Zey made 'oles and some footprints in ze nice green lawn. Ze police found zat zey 'ad trampled over ze strawberry-bed and gobbled up some of ze fruit – ze strawberries zat zey didn't eat 'ad been squashed by zeir big feet.' The children laughed heartily. 'Zey 'ad been up trees too, and sent showers of leaves down on top of all ze flowers. When ze police arrived zey were asleep in ze sun on top of ze roof and 'ad to be coaxed down wiz bananas. Just now zey are in ze summer-'ouse – my wife will not 'ave zem in 'er clean 'ome. We 'ave offered to look after zem, and zen take zem along to ze ferry at eleven.'

'Oooh! Are they coming on the ferry with us?' Jack enquired eagerly.

'Yes. Zere will be a van waiting for zem in England at ze 'arbour to take zem to ze circus. It 'as all been arranged.'

Mrs Pompidou showed the children their photographs in her French newspaper. There was masses of writing about them, and even a small picture of Jessica. The children laughed at the ridiculous face she was pulling.

Even though they were going home, it was sad to leave the kind Pompidous who had done so much for them. The children politely thanked the family, who said it was a pleasure to have helped them. Louis was driving them to the harbour in his car. He didn't mind having Jessica and Gepetto in the back, but Jack and Anna needed to hold the restless chimpanzees so that they would keep still and not distract Louis while he was driving.

Some policemen were waiting at the harbour to escort the children, and apes, on to the ferry. Louis introduced the children to his friend, Captain Durand, who was taking care of them during the voyage. Jessica and Gepetto loved the boat but had to be kept out of mischief. Everyone aboard was very friendly towards the children because, of course, they had heard all about the hero and heroines. The chimpanzees thoroughly enjoyed all the fuss that people made over them. Captain Durand was very kind to Jack, Sarah and Anna. He showed them all round the boat, and they were able to watch the engine working. The Captain provided them with lunch at midday and produced fruit for the apes.

It did not take long to get to England. As the ferry slid into the harbour at Dover, people gathered on the pier, cheering. The children wondered why! Then, as they disembarked, they realized it was because of *them*. More interviewers and photographers crowded round, and camera bulbs flashed while microphones bobbed about under the children's noses and men asked, 'Would you tell us something about your adventure for BBC news?' It was all very exciting, but, of course, when they caught sight of their parents waving and trying to squeeze through the crowds, the children didn't stop for any more photographs or interviews. Sarah's mother wasn't there, naturally, but much to the girl's surprise Mr

Interviewers and photographers crowded round

Thomas was waiting with his wife to welcome her.
He had very kindly driven Anna's Pa and Ma down
to the seaport to meet their daughter. What a
gorgeous surprise it was for Anna! Mr and Mrs
Wilton embraced their son and showed how glad
they were to have him back. Yvonne jumped around
her brother excitedly. Meanwhile Mr Thomas was
saying to the amazed Sarah, 'My dear! We are *so*
glad you are safe. Ah! How lovely it is to see you
again! I do apologize for the way I behaved when
you were still with us. My! What an adventure you
and your friends have had!'

With a babble of voices all around them, the
children were led to Mr Wilton's car and Mr
Thomas' cream-coloured one. A van was waiting for
Jessica and Gepetto who were lifted inside, sorry to
leave all the friendly people, and the peanuts which
an affectionate little boy had been feeding to them.

The crowds cheered as the two cars moved off and
a few camera bulbs flashed for the last time. Soon
Dover was far behind them. After about an hour,
they were travelling through busy London, heading
for the countryside beyond. The chimpanzees' van
trundled along behind. All the vehicles stopped
outside the Thomases' house, with Molly, Billy and
Mark dancing about on the pavement. Then, while
Jack was being driven home with his family in his
father's car, Molly led Anna and her parents
through the Thomases' home to the circus field.
There were screams of delight and to Anna's surprise music began. Circus children in their best
attire rushed over to offer her sweets and fruit. She

was led to a big fire where a delicious meal of meat was roasting. All the circus folk were gathered there wearing their fancy costumes. Even old Mr Morgan had come out of his caravan to greet Anna. The wagons were decorated with wreaths of flowers and some were hung with banners saying, 'WELCOME BACK, ANNA!' and 'OUR HEROINE IS BACK!' and 'WELL DONE, ANNA!' The bewildered girl could not believe that this was all for her. She had not known how much the circus folk admired and cared about her. In the midst of all the excitement, Gepetto and Jessica were led in. 'Hurrah!' cried the circus folk, and ran to fondle the chimpanzees. They were sorry Lianio could not return to them but would employ a new trainer for the dear apes. Soon they settled down again and ate their meal while Anna told of the adventure yet again. But she was so tired – would you believe it? – that she fell asleep in the middle of the tale. Her Pa carried her to his caravan and laid his daughter on her bed.

Meantime, Sarah had gone into the Thomases' house with Molly, Billy and Mark and their parents. While she had been away, a cable had come from Canada to announce that her mother would be returning that very day. Mrs Parkinson's arrival was expected any minute now, so Sarah sat eagerly watching at the window and told the Thomases her story at the same time. Just as she reached the bit where they had got through the secret tunnel into the first dungeon – a taxi stopped at the garden gate with Mrs Parkinson inside. Sarah's legs couldn't carry her fast enough as she swept past the front door and into her mother's outstretched arms.

'Hello, darling! It's so lovely to see you!'

'Hello, Mummy! How are you? Is Aunt Harriet quite, quite better now?'

'Oh yes! She's fine. And how have you been getting on?' Mrs Parkinson had obviously not heard about the adventure yet.

'Oooh Mother! I went to France and found treasure.'

Mrs Parkinson looked bewildered. 'You did?'

'Yes,' put in Mrs Thomas. 'I think you'd better come inside. Sarah has something to tell you.'

'Oh – er – please hold on a second.' Sarah's mother turned to the taxi and Sarah saw for the first time that there was another man inside apart from the driver. The man stepped out. He had a pleasant face and friendly blue eyes.

'This is Mr Marsh,' said Mrs Parkinson, taking the man's hand. 'I met him in Canada and he has been very kind to me. He drove me to and from the hospital each day in his car, and bought flowers and grapes for Aunt Harriet.' Mrs Parkinson paused. 'So – er – to cut a long story short – we have decided to get married, dear, and you shall have a father at last.' I expect you can guess how happy Sarah was. It was like a dream come true. Mr Marsh had a kind face, so like Jack's that it made Sarah like him even more.

She woke up late next morning after staying up long past her bedtime the night before to tell her mother and Mr Marsh all about the adventure. She felt extremely happy and it was lovely to wake up in her own pretty room.

Two days later there was yet another surprise for Sarah. A large white envelope arrived containing a money order for fifty pounds and a letter saying:

'We are very grateful to you for your help in finding the treasure and capturing the wanted criminals. Therefore we are enclosing an order for fifty pounds which we hope you shall enjoy spending.'

It was from the French museum which had the Dubarry treasure. Of course, Sarah was delighted. So were Anna and Jack who had each received the same reward. Jack bought himself a grand bicycle which he used a great deal, especially for scouting round the countryside.

Anna had never *seen* so much money as fifty pounds, let alone possessed it. She decided to buy what she wanted most – and that was a sealion. Anna's heart burst with joy when she saw the sleek black creature waddling towards her for the first time. Anna called him Frisky, and it didn't take long before the little sealion could balance a ball on his nose.

Sarah knew what to buy as soon as she received the money. She was going to get her parents a splendid wedding present. After much careful thought, she decided on a set of crystal wine glasses with delicate flower designs cut into them.

She was very excited when the wedding day came. All of the Thomases, the Wiltons and Anna's family had been invited. It was indeed a very enjoyable occasion. After the ceremony in church, there came the reception. Everyone gathered round the trestle table which was spread with a delicious feast. While the adults drank a toast to the wedded pair, Jack lifted his glass of lemonade before Sarah and Anna, calling heartily, 'Cheers, girls! Here's to another adventure! May it be as wonderfully exciting as this has been!'